JOIN THE NEWSLETTER FOR UPDATES

*W*ant a free bonus scene from Quoth's point of view? Grab a free copy of *Cabinet of Curiosities* – a Steffanie Holmes compendium of short stories and bonus scenes – when you sign up for updates with the Steffanie Holmes newsletter.

www.steffanieholmes.com/newsletter

Every week in my newsletter I talk about the true-life hauntings, strange happenings, crumbling ruins, and creepy facts that inspire my stories. You'll also get newsletter-exclusive bonus scenes and updates. I love to talk to my readers, so come join us for some spooky fun :)

CRIME AND PUBLISHING

NEVERMORE BOOKSHOP MYSTERIES, BOOK 8

STEFFANIE HOLMES

BACCHANALIA HOUSE

CRIME AND PUBLISHING

The pen is deadlier than the sword, especially when it's filled with poison.

Mina Wilde is thrilled to be invited to a prestigious writers' retreat at Meddleworth House. Heathcliff, Morrie, and Quoth decide to come along to keep her company and indulge in some of the estate's many activities.

Mina is excited to get feedback on her first novel, but her dreams of writing stardom are shattered when the other writers tear her work to pieces. A little criticism never hurt anyone, right?

Wrong.

Their picturesque country holiday soon turns deadly when a violent storm closes in. As the writers gather around the fire to critique each other's work, the power goes out. When the lights come back on, they discover one of them has been murdered by his own pen!

The only people who could have possibly committed this crime were the other writers, and with no way in or out of the manor house, Mina throws herself into solving this locked room mystery. But as our favorite sleuth eliminates her suspects, she must face a terrifying truth.

There *are* three other people who could have got into the room and committed the murder – her boyfriends. How far will Morrie, Quoth, and Heathcliff go to save Mina's literary reputation?

For readers everywhere who like their tea the way they like their books: shamelessly purchased for a burst of brain sunshine even though you're got stacks of perfectly decent flavors at home.

Yet if hope has flown away
In a night, or in a day,
In a vision, or in none,
Is it therefore the less gone?
All that we see or seem
Is but a dream within a dream.

Edgar Allen Poe, 'A Dream Within a Dream', 1849

CHAPTER ONE

Bree: Mina, have an amazing time at
Meddleworth House! I've just arrived at the shop
and I got your list, and I promise that I definitely
won't go into the cellar or open the room at the
end of the hallway in the flat.

Is it okay if Pax, Edward, and Ambrose stay with
me for the week? They've promised to be on
their best behavior, and I don't want to leave
them alone at Grimwood Manor or I'll come back
to find the place burned down.

J spoke into my phone to send a reply to Bree, then
looked up with a start as my head slammed into the
roof of the car.

"I may be blind, but I'm pretty sure we're no longer driving on
a road."

"Relax, gorgeous." The world's foremost criminal mastermind
leaned over the wheel as the tiny electric car bumped down a
terrifyingly steep slope. "I am in complete control of this vehicle."

"That's what I'm afraid of," I muttered as we lurched to the
side, our wheels spinning on the slick ground beneath us.

"Arf!" Oscar rested his head on my knees and placed his paw on my arm, trying to calm me down.

Calm? What was calm? I hadn't been calm since the day I received the letter inviting me to the famous Meddleworth House Crime Writers Retreat – but that was more due to excitement than my current state of terror for my life. I finished my first manuscript a few months ago and I'd been reading and re-reading it, trying to make it perfect. That and wandering aimlessly around Nevermore Bookshop, running my fingers along the spines of my favorite books and imagining my own work joining their ranks.

I, Mina Wilde, former fashion designer, bookstore co-owner, mystery solver extraordinaire, vampire-slayer, lover of three fictional men, and blind girl about town, was on a mission to become a published author.

Hopefully.

If I could impress Hugh Briston this week.

Hugh Briston was the managing editor of Red Herring Press and *the* expert on British crime writing. One word from Briston to the literary community would make or break a crime writer. I wanted him to make me.

Which was why I was so desperate to impress him on the retreat. My three boyfriends decided to come along to Meddleworth House to keep me company. When I would be busy in the daily writing and critique sessions, Morrie would be at the spa getting scrubbed, wrapped, and rubbed. Heathcliff would be in the library glowering at anyone who dared disturb his calm. And Quoth would be taking a painting class in the art studio, getting ideas for his own gallery, and chatting with the (hopefully) friendly local ravens.

They'd been almost as excited about the trip as me, which was why Morrie in his infinite wisdom decided that he would finally go and get his driver's license so he could drive us to the estate in style. He was so proud of his new car – a cute little Nissan Leaf –

but so far we'd all refused to get inside with him on account of the stack of speeding and parking tickets that have darkened Nevermore's letterbox since he got it.

But Meddleworth was in the middle of nowhere in Yorkshire, so we didn't have a choice. We crammed the four of us, our overnight bags, my laptop and Braille note, Quoth's art supplies, and Oscar into the tiny car and set off with a due sense of trepidation.

The drive had been relatively uneventful so far, but that might have been because I was sitting in the front seat and I no longer had enough vision left to see how fast we were going or how many near misses we had. But even I knew that when Morrie declared, "This is a shortcut to the manor," and turned down a steep dirt track, we were in trouble.

"Morrie, there's a river," Quoth's voice trembled from the backseat, where he was balancing a box of paints in his lap. "You're driving us directly into a *river.*"

"Good." I heard Heathcliff turn a page in his book. "If I drown, I won't have to listen to any more of Mina's playlist."

"This is Lydia Lunch's *Queen of Siam* album," I shot back. "It's highly influential for combining jazz with punk—"

"To create junk?"

Morrie laughed.

"You're such a heathen," I glowered over my shoulder at him. "What do you want to put on next, then? Some Madrigal Singers? Kate Bush screaming about your dead girlfriend—"

"Guys, the river!" Quoth's voice wobbled.

The car bounced over something hard and launched into the air. I cried out as we jiggled several times, kicking up river stones as we hurtled toward doom.

"Don't worry," Morrie said with way more confidence than he should possess at this moment. "The guy who sold me this car said it could go anywhere. We'll be fine."

"Did he say it had sails?" Heathcliff asked in a bored voice. "Because you should unfurl them now."

Oscar whimpered as the car hit the ground again and juddered over the rough earth. I became aware of the roar of moving water somewhere nearby. I leaned down and punched the button to raise my window.

"Morrie, are you sure this is the right way—"

"Hold your breath!" Quoth yelled. "We're going in!"

"Relax," Morrie grumbled. "Everything is fi—"

His words cut off with a yell as the car plowed into a raging river.

CHAPTER TWO

"It's deeper than I thought." Morrie yanked the steering wheel, but the car didn't pay any attention. It rolled and bumped over the river stones as it floated deeper into the water. My ears rang with the roar of rushing water as the force of the river battered the car. The current turned it in a half circle and sent a wave of icy water over the windshield and through Morrie's open window.

"Argh!" Morrie jerked back as the water soaked him and splashed through the vehicle. Oscar howled and climbed onto my lap. I yanked my legs out of the footwell as icy water poured in.

The front of the car dipped forward, and more water cascaded through the window. The car made a sickening groaning sound, and a disconcerting fizzing noise rose from beneath the bonnet.

Morrie said, "I don't think batteries are supposed to get wet…"

"I always assumed I was going to drink myself to death after one too many customers asks me if Nigella Lawson's books are shelved under cookery or erotica," Heathcliff said drolly from the back. "I'm so grateful Morrie proved me wrong."

No. This is not going to be how I die.

"I think," Morrie said in a small voice, "we're going to have to abandon ship."

"Nobody panic. I'll save the whisky." I heard the clink of a bottle as Heathcliff shoved his 16-year Fettercairn down his trousers. He slammed his weight against his door. "It won't budge. The water pressure on the other side is too great."

"I read that you have to open the door a little at a time and allow the water to flow into the car," Quoth said as he flung my backpack and his paints over his shoulder and reached for his own door. "Once the pressure is equalized, the door should push open easier."

"Got it." Heathcliff shoved his door again, and managed to open it an inch. Freezing water poured in, filling his footwell and sending the car lurching.

"You read up on how to save yourself from a drowning vehicle?" I shoved Oscar onto Morrie's lap so I could find my seatbelt.

"Well, Morrie was driving us, so I thought it would be wise."

Morrie, meanwhile, had managed to squeeze his lanky frame out of his open window. The fizzing sound got worse, and was now accentuated by some loud POPs. Morrie knelt on top of the car and extended a hand down. "I've got you, gorgeous."

I gave Oscar a shove toward the window as the water started to lap at the bottom of the seats. "Go on, boy. Go to Morrie. You like swimming, don't you?"

Oscar didn't need to be told twice. He leaped through the window and hit the water, paddling in a determined circle as he turned back to help me. I winced as I put my foot down into the footwell and the ice-cold water stabbed at the bare skin of my ankle. I'd worn a peasant dress covered in skulls for the drive, and a new pair of soft suede boots that were now probably ruined.

"Argh!" I jolted forward as water splashed through Heathcliff's door and trickled down my back. More water poured in through the window, soaking my clothes as I clambered across the seats and grabbed Morrie's hand. He pulled me through the window. I stood on the window as water splashed around my feet, and the car lurched horribly, my heart hammering. We were going to flip over or sink at any moment.

But we didn't. Morrie pulled me up onto the roof of the car. My teeth chattered as I bunched up my soaking skirt. A moment later, Heathcliff hauled himself up alongside us.

"What do we do now?" Even with my poor vision, I could see that we were out in the middle of the raging river, with both banks impossibly far away.

One of my suitcases bobbed past, followed by Heathcliff, who had slid off the roof and was frantically swimming after it, his rucksack and Morrie's fancy leather satchel strapped to his back.

"Honestly, I hadn't thought that far ahead." Morrie whipped his head around. "Quoth, did your book have any advice on what to do now that we're out of the car?"

"Croak?" A raven cried as it soared overhead.

Wait there, Quoth's voice landed in my ears. *The current is too strong to swim against. I'm going to try and find a rope.*

"Great. That's just great," Morrie pulled me into his chest, rubbing my shivering shoulders as the car dropped another few inches in the water. "We're trapped on a sinking vessel and the bird has just flown away on a wild raven chase—"

"Hullo there!" a bright, deep voice called out. "You seem to be in a spot of bother. Do you need some help?"

CHAPTER THREE

I looked over at the bank where the voice had come from, but I couldn't see what was going on. Steam was now rising from the car's bonnet, and the fizzing and popping sounds were so loud they nearly drowned out the other voice.

"There's a fellow over there with a big bushy beard," Morrie said. "He's helping Heathcliff out of the water. And he has a four-wheel-drive vehicle and…is that a…"

Something hit the side of the vehicle. I yelped in surprise. Morrie flailed for something but cursed as he missed.

"I'm gonna throw the rope again," the man called out. "Can ye grab it?"

"Is it silk rope?" Morrie yelled back. "Because these hands require something soft and supple, made only of natural fibers—"

"Just shut up and do what he says," Heathcliff growled from the shore.

Morrie crawled to the opposite side of the car. I could hear him grunting as the rope splashed into the water. "Again!" he called out. "I just have to stretch a little further."

"Croak," Quoth cried out. I whirled around and could just

make out a dark shape swoop through the air, grab the rope by the talons, and drop it into Morrie's outstretched hand.

"Thanks, ye strange bird!" the man called out.

Just save Mina! Quoth's voice sang inside my head as he landed on the bank. He was talking to Heathcliff. *I don't care about the other one.*

"Hey!" Morrie cried out, but he looped the rope around his stomach. "Mina, climb on my shoulders and hold on. No matter what happens, you have to hold on. Do you think Oscar can keep this end of the rope in his mouth?"

"Oscar can do anything."

"Okay, then. Here we go."

Morrie slid off the roof of the car and into the current. I gasped as the chilly water rose around me. I tightened my grip around Morrie's neck as the current grabbed us, tugging us downstream. Morrie looped the rope around his middle and gave the end to Oscar, who bit down like a champ.

I held onto Morrie for dear life as he and Oscar dog-paddled toward the shore as Heathcliff and the strange man pulled the rope in, hand over hand. When we got close enough that Morrie could stand on the bottom, he was able to move us faster.

Heathcliff waded out and hauled me off Morrie's shoulders, carrying me in his strong arms and depositing me lovingly on the bank. Oscar bounded out of the water and shook himself off. He barked with happiness, keen to head out again for another swim.

"Take my hand," Heathcliff yelled at Morrie, who was still standing waist-deep in the water.

"I think I'll stay out here, actually," Morrie said nervously, his voice hoarse. He must have been exhausted from the effort of getting that far. "I'll wait till erosion takes me to the castle gates. It seems safer than dealing with your wrath."

"For pity's sake," Heathcliff muttered. Morrie yelped, and I could see from the vague shape of them that Heathcliff had thrown Morrie over his shoulder and was climbing out of the water. He deposited a damp and sheepish Morrie beside me just as Quoth emerged from the bushes and perched on my shoulder. The stranger watched us with amusement as he coiled the rope over his arm.

"Arf!" Oscar butted the stranger's hand, as if to thank him for his valiant efforts.

"Thank you for saving us." I turned to our rescuer. "I can't believe our luck that you happened to be nearby. We thought we were in the middle of nowhere."

"Not at all. You're actually only a couple of miles from Meddleworth House. I happened to see this little fella swooping around and thought it odd, as the estate's ravens are housed near the buildings. I thought one had escaped, so I stopped, and that's when I heard you yelling." He tipped his hat at me. "My name's Jonathan. Jonathan Marley Norgrove. I'm the groundskeeper, bellhop, security guard, and general dogsbody here at the estate."

"Mina Wilde." I extended my hand. "We're actually guests at Meddleworth. I'm here for the writer's retreat."

"And Morrie's here for driving lessons," Heathcliff cut in.

Jonathan laughed deep in his belly. "Never ye mind about that. T'was an honest mistake. Ye were following an old maintenance track. If you'd driven this way a month ago, you wouldn't have had a problem. But we've been having some terrible storms lately and the water table is high, so the stream at the back of the property has overflowed and diverted here." He patted my shoulder. "In fact, judging by those clouds overhead, I should get you up to the manor before we get caught in the next downpour."

"What about the car?" Morrie asked, his voice strained.

Jonathan started to say something, but he was interrupted by a mighty *BOOM*.

I slammed my hands over my ears jerked back as a plume of water shot out of the river, and mangled bits of car rained back down into the water. The air reeked of burning, and I could no longer see the jaunty bonnet of the Leaf bobbing in the water.

"I don't think yee have to worry about the car anymore, lad," Jonathan said.

"What happened?" I asked, a chill running down my spine as I realized that without Jonathon's help, we might've still be trapped in the car when it exploded.

"Morrie happened," Heathcliff said. "Poor Leaf. It didn't deserve such a cruel end."

"The batteries must've caught fire," Jonathan said. "Electric, was she? A load of modern nonsense, if you ask me. A good old-fashioned diesel engine would have got you across that river no trouble. I'll come back after I've got ye all settled in, see if I can fish the main bits out of the river. At least you saved your luggage – there will be enough room for all of ye in my range rover. Come on up the path, steady as she goes." Jonathan supported me as Oscar and I shuffled around a fallen log. "We don't want any more accidents now."

We certainly did not.

I wiped my sodden hair out of my eyes as my wet skirt slapped against my bare, shivering knees.

Our weeklong holiday at Meddleworth was off to a...*predictable* start.

CHAPTER FOUR

Bree: Mina, when you get a chance, give me a call. I can't see Grimalkin anywhere.

She hasn't come for her dinner.

It's possible the ghosts scared her away, but ducks are normally the animals who can see spirits, not cats. (Don't ask me, I don't make the rules.)

I figure she's probably sleeping somewhere, but I want to check on her. Anywhere she might be hiding?

*H*eathcliff picked up all the bags and we followed Jonathan a short way along the muddy maintenance track and piled into his enormous range rover. We drove through a beautiful wood to emerge on the edge of a wide lawn, laid out with neat rows of parterre gardens and a long, rectangular pool that had overflowed its concrete border. Wide, deep puddles reflected the grim, grey skies.

"There she is, Meddleworth House." Jonathan grinned as he gestured to a towering edifice of grey stone that I assumed was the castle. Meddleworth was technically a castle, and it still had the original gatehouse and some crumbling curtain walls (although we hadn't got to see them thanks to Morrie's shortcut), but it had been converted into a stately home in the seventeenth century. I'd had Quoth describe the pictures to me, and I knew it was a long building finished in the Italianate style by Sir Charles Barry with its low-pitched roof, projecting eaves, imposing carved cornices and pediments, and a plethora of romantic loggias and balconies. All I could make out now was the faint outline of the impressive building, but it was enough to form an impression.

Plus, I bet it was warm.

It's beautiful, Quoth whispered inside my head, his talons digging into my shoulder. I knew he hadn't intended to show up at Meddleworth in his bird form, but his clothes were now somewhere at the bottom of the river, and if he shifted now, he'd make quite an impression.

Jonathan parked up around the corner beside an old outbuilding and started off across the muddy lawn, walking at a brisk pace. Morrie's long legs had no trouble keeping up with him, and Heathcliff walked with me and Oscar, laden down with all our bags. Quoth took off, telling us that he'd meet us in the room later.

"Have you worked here long?" Morrie asked Jonathan.

"Aye, for most of my life. My father was the old groundskeeper, back when this was still a stately home and the Bollstead family were—" he trailed off, then scratched his head. "Let's say that things have changed around here with Donna's new innovations."

He said innovations like it was a dirty word. I assumed he was talking about the luxury spa that the current owner, Donna Bollstead, had installed. Personally, I was hoping I'd be able to find an hour or so away from the retreat where I could try one of the treatments.

Oscar, of course, thought it was a grand game to walk me through the puddles. By the time we reached the castle, we were cold, muddy, and miserable.

But that changed the moment Jonathan flung open the doors and ushered us inside. The entrance foyer was lit by an enormous, glittering chandelier that drew my eyes immediately. Warmth from a roaring fire permeated my bones. We made our way squelchily around the perimeter of the room so I could learn the space, and Jonathan stopped at every suit of armor, gilded portrait, and sword display to tell us about the history of the place. He was a walking Meddleworth guidebook.

"When my father was a boy, he once hid in this suit of armor." Jonathan rapped his knuckles lovingly on a shiny set beside the reception desk. "It was during one of the infamous Meddleworth writing retreats, and the famed poet Caspian Steele was complaining loudly about a cockroach in his shower when the knight's hand stretched out toward him, beckoning him from beyond the grave. Caspian ran out of the hotel and never came back. He wrote a poem about the day – one of his best, although I'm no judge; I don't really understand poetry. But it's hanging on the wall in the restaurant…"

Jonathan ducked his head into the restaurant, where staff members were bustling about, preparing the tables for tonight's literary feast. Although only four writers were attending the retreat, the reception drew people from the publishing world from all over the country. My chest flipped with excitement. I was going to meet some of my literary idols tonight.

And hopefully, my future colleagues.

I hope I brought the right outfit.

"Arf!" Oscar reassured me as he trotted after Jonathan.

"Guest rooms are on floors one and two of the south wing," Jonathan explained as he led us up a carved, winding staircase. "Below is the restaurant and the conference rooms and library and drawing rooms where the retreat will be held. In the north wing, you'll find the spa and gym and meditation room, as well as the art studio in the old servants' quarters, and the pottery workshop and forge in the outbuildings."

Morrie rubbed his hands together gleefully, apparently already forgetting about the harrowing experience he'd just put us all through. "I'm looking forward to being oiled."

Jonathan pushed a door open and ushered us inside. The room was enormous, with whitewashed walls, huge stone lintels, and heavy, antique wooden furniture. I loved it instantly. "Here is your suite. You have these two rooms with a view over the grounds. Isn't there a fourth member of your party?"

"Er, yes." I leaned against the window just as Quoth fluttered down and perched on the sill. "He's...arriving separately."

"I hope he gets in soon. We're due for another thunderstorm tomorrow night, and the weather is going to start getting worse in an hour or so."

"He'll be here," I said. "He didn't try to take a shortcut."

Morrie held his hand over his heart and flopped onto the bed. "Ow, gorgeous, I'm bleeding."

Jonathan cracked another smile. "Well, I shall leave ye to get settled. We don't have laundry facilities onsite, but you can dry your clothes by the fire. I'll go pull the rest of your car out of the river."

"Thanks, Jonathan. We're so sorry for the trouble."

"No trouble at all. Nothing is too much trouble for guests at Meddleworth." Jonathan nodded as he exited the room.

As soon as the door shut I whirled around and let Quoth inside. He hopped down onto the floor and transformed into his human form.

"Brrrr." He ran his hands through his damp hair. "There's a real chill in the air out there. I think Jonathan's right – a serious storm is coming."

"You flew away from us when we were crossing the lawn.

What did you see?" I asked Quoth as I started to peel off my ruined boots and squelchy socks.

"Ravens!" His voice trembled with wonder. "Down there beside the house. I can hear at least four of them, but I couldn't see them from the air. Do you think I—"

"Go. I don't need you for anything. Jonathan thinks you're arriving later, anyway. Just be back here before we leave for dinner so you can change."

Quoth kissed me on the cheek. "Thank you."

I kept my hand on his shoulder as he transformed again. I loved feeling the way Quoth's body shifted and changed – the bones rearranging themselves, his muscles twisting, the thick, soft black feathers punching through his skin.

Ever since the bookshop's magic pulled him through into our world and made him this creature that could change forms, Quoth has thought himself an aberration – something that should not exist. But to me, he was a miracle.

A moment later, an enormous black bird with a distinctive frill around his neck hopped across the floor in front of me. He unfurled his wings and soared through the window, and I shut it behind him, blocking out the frigid air. I picked up Oscar's harness again and wandered into the adjoining bedroom, where Morrie had already laid open our sodden suitcases and was inspecting his shirts.

"Thankfully, most of our clothing has survived unscathed." Morrie hung up his designer clothing and glanced at the fancy watch on his wrist.

"Speak for yourself." Heathcliff tossed soaking shirts from his battered old rucksack into a pile in front of the fireplace.

"I told you that you need to invest in decent luggage." Morrie unbuttoned his wet shirt. "We have an hour until dinner. I hope that's enough time to make me look presentable as the boyfriend of a soon-to-be bestselling author."

"We don't know that," I said, trying to temper their enthusiasm even as my own heart pattered in my chest. "It's the first book I've written and I don't know if it's any good—"

"I thought it was brilliant." Heathcliff flicked a dark, damp curl from his forehead as he pulled a small leatherbound book from a compartment in his rucksack – seemingly the only part of his luggage that was waterproof. "And I have impeccable taste."

"You do, but unfortunately, it's Hugh Briston I need to impress." I stepped out of my sodden peasant dress and flopped down on the bed to sort through the clothes I brought along, hunting for the dress I'd chosen for tonight. "But he must have liked it if he invited me to the retreat. Do you know that every year he offers one member of the retreat a publishing contract with Red Herring Press? I'm trying not to get my hopes up, but my hopes are already soaring away with Quoth."

"So what's the deal tonight?" Heathcliff closed his book with a sigh. He knew what I was like when I was excited. I wouldn't be able to stop talking and fidgeting, and Morrie would only encourage me.

"The retreat members and their partners are invited to attend a reception with Hugh and select invited writers and publishing people in the music room, before a sit-down dinner. I already RSVPed for all of us."

"Mina's memorized the entire week's schedule," Morrie said with a knowing smirk in his voice.

"I have not." My cheeks burned with heat.

I totally had.

My phone buzzed in my purse. I lunged at it, but Heathcliff kicked my purse out of the way.

"Don't answer it," Heathcliff growled.

"But I—"

"You're supposed to be on *holiday*."

"It's probably Bree. The shop's burning down and she—"

"If the shop is burning down, there's nothing you can do about it from here. Live in ignorance and enjoy it." Heathcliff glared at my purse, which was now vibrating its way across the rug.

"It could be my mother."

"All the more reason to avoid answering it."

"Maybe you're right." Mum had recently started creating and selling her own NFTs. Hers were photographs of Grimalkin sleeping in various strange and unusual places around the bookshop. One person had purchased one with some weird cryptocurrency, and now Mum thought she'd make a fortune. She didn't even know how to cash in her crypto for actual money. I don't know how Grimalkin put up with being posed and photographed all the time, but my grandmother had been sleeping more than usual lately. Either way, my mother's interest in cryptocurrency was a new source of stress in my life, and Heathcliff was right in that it was nice not to have her and her phone camera underfoot.

"Of course I'm right." Heathcliff patted his knee. "Come here and rejoice in the fact that for a whole week, you are far away from Helen Wilde's insanity."

Even though I was desperate for a hot shower and to start getting ready, I couldn't resist that deep, gravelly voice. I crossed the floor and settled down on his knee. Heathcliff had removed his wet trousers, and his damp skin was warm against mine as he wrapped his arms around me and tucked me into his shoulder. He was sitting on an enormous, egg-shaped chair facing a fireplace containing a modern gas fire, and the chair cocooned us both. In this little corner, it really did feel like nothing in the real world mattered anymore.

Heathcliff pulled me into one of his bone-crushing hugs. I breathed in his spicy, peaty scent. I loved the way he held me like this, so tight that nothing or no one could separate us. "I can't believe we're not in Argleton anymore."

"Good riddance." Heathcliff pressed his lips to my forehead, his beard brushing my skin. "I'm pleased to see the back of that dump."

I raised an eyebrow. "This from the same Heathcliff who only says 'morning' to people, because if you were having a 'good morning,' then you'd be in bed and not talking to people."

"Don't worry." Heathcliff tapped the book he'd discarded on the arm of the chair. "I fully intend to ignore people here, too."

"As long as you're on-brand."

"Hey, look at this." I glanced over my shoulder as Morrie held up something square and white from my suitcase. He held it closer, and I realized it was the stack of manuscripts I'd printed off. I'd made my notes on them digitally and printed them off to exchange with the other writers. "No wonder my car didn't make it across the river. Mina was weighing us down with *War and Peace* over here."

"That's not *War and Peace*. It's the excerpts from the other writers' novels. I had to mark them up with my notes as part of the retreat."

And I was nervous about that part of the retreat, too. I'd never done anything like that before. And tomorrow I'd find out what they thought about my book. My very *personal* book about a blind amateur sleuth who solved mysteries with her three boyfriends who were all famous men from literature...

My stomach twisted. What if they hated it? How was I going to survive this weekend?

Maybe I'm not cut out to be a writer...

Heathcliff must have sensed what I was feeling, because he always did. He knew me better than I knew myself. He squeezed me tighter and brushed his lips across my forehead again. "Whatever they say about you, remember that you're Mina Wilde and you're *our* heroine."

My chest fluttered at his words. I squeezed him back. "I'll try. I'm so nervous I don't even know if I'll be able to eat tonight. I wish I could stop thinking about it."

"Do you want to know what I'm thinking about right now?" Heathcliff's deep voice rumbled against my earlobe.

"What?"

"I'm thinking about how the rain has made that bra of yours cling in *all* the right places."

His hand swiped up my side, his fingers dancing over the damp fabric of my bra to brush my nipple, which was already hard from the cold. It stiffened and tingled beneath his touch.

And suddenly, I wasn't thinking about manuscript critiques any longer.

Heathcliff tipped my head back and claimed my mouth with his. Gone were the nerves about meeting the acclaimed publisher in an hour. All that mattered were Heathcliff's demanding lips on mine and his body melting around me.

"We only have an hour until dinner..." I moaned as he pushed up my sodden bra to stroke the rough pad of his thumb over my nipple.

"I don't need an hour. I'm perfectly dressed for dinner."

I threw one leg over his and rearranged myself so I was straddling him. Even though Heathcliff was a beast of a man, there was plenty of room for both of us in the chair. He groaned against me, thrusting his hips up to grind his hardness between my legs. Only the thin fabric of my panties separated us. We were both still dripping wet from our swim in the river and the subsequent drizzle, but it was nothing on the wetness I could feel soaking my panties as Heathcliff deepened the kiss.

Kissing Heathcliff was like throwing yourself over a cliff. It was falling into darkness with his arms around you, knowing, believing, that he would always be there to catch you. Heathcliff's hand cupped the column of my throat and he drew me deeper, sending a surge of warmth through my body.

My fingers fumbled with the buttons of his sodden black shirt, popping them open one by one and tossing the offending fabric in the general direction of the bed.

"What gives?" Morrie yelled. I must've hit him with the shirt, but then he'd turned and saw us because he said, "Ah, I see." And a moment later, he bent over the chair, his chest pressed against my back and his teeth scraped along my collarbone.

"Let us get you out of these wet clothes, gorgeous." Morrie's hands stroked the sensitive undersides of my arms as he unhooked my bra and tossed it away. Heathcliff's lips never left mine, his kiss deep and needy, and his fingers teased and rolled my nipples until I was ready to beg for more.

Morrie – who did so love to be in control of these things – scraped his fingers down Heathcliff's chest, leaving scratch marks that made Heathcliff shudder with pleasure. Morrie picked up Heathcliff's belt from where he'd tossed it beside the fire.

"I could do all sorts of filthy things with this," Morrie whispered against my earlobe as he trailed the tip of the leather belt down my naked back. I shivered with anticipation, but then Morrie tossed it over his shoulder. "Unfortunately, we don't have time for all my games. I think we have just enough time to make Mina scream."

"We'd have even more time if you stopped talking," Heathcliff growled against my lips. His hands roamed everywhere on my body.

"Why don't you make me, Lord Bossybritches?"

With a growl, Heathcliff grabbed Morrie's cheeks and yanked his head forward. His lips left mine to kiss Morrie. I rested my head on Morrie's shoulder, watching as Heathcliff devoured him, feeling Morrie's heart race against his chest. Morrie had been burning a candle for Heathcliff for a long time, longer than I've known them, and for all his arrogance he still couldn't believe that what they had – what we had – was real.

I didn't blame him. Sometimes – like now – my heart hurt from the sheer joy of having these men in my life and knowing they were mine.

After all this time, it still thrilled me to see them kiss. I'd fallen hard for both of them since the very first day I started working in the shop, and there was nothing that made a person happier than seeing someone you loved truly find themselves. I got to have the three of them, so why shouldn't Heathcliff and Morrie explore this thing that had unfurled between them?

All four of us loved each other in our own ways. And I couldn't ask for anything more honest or beautiful from our relationship.

While the two of them got out their pent-up emotions by devouring each other's lips, I worked open Heathcliff's boxers. I reached inside and pulled out his length, running my fingers down the silken skin of his rather large and very hard cock.

Heathcliff's groans of pleasure spurred me on. He battled against Morrie's wanton tongue while I stroked him slowly, until his tip jerked in my hand, glistening with pre-cum. A warm, delicious ache welled up inside me that had nothing to do with imminent dinner.

"This chair was practically made for us," I observed as I rose up on my knees and shuffled forward, shoving his boxers down further and fitting myself perfectly over Heathcliff's cock.

I sighed as I sank down onto him. He was so big and so hard that it hurt a little...in the best possible way. I wriggled my hips, pushing him deeper, as deep as he could go.

I rose up on my knees, slowly, deliciously slowly, feeling him slide out of me, relishing the delicious ache of his absence. And then I dropped my body weight, sheathing him inside me, filling myself up with him until I couldn't take anymore.

Morrie broke from his kiss to watch. "That's it, gorgeous. You ride him like he needs to learn a lesson."

I rose up again, opening my body to every sensation; the warmth of Morrie's chest pressed against mine, the strength of Heathcliff's thigh muscles as mine squeezed him, the ragged rush of his breath against my skin.

As I slid down onto him again, Heathcliff cupped my cheek

with his hand. I loved when he did this – his hands were so large and powerful, I believe he could crush a skull if he felt like it. But he made me feel safe in a way I never could have imagined.

His lips crushed mine as he wrested control from me, bucking his thighs to thrust deeper inside me. Fucking Heathcliff was such a wild experience. He demanded everything, every part of you. More than your body, he demanded your mind, your heart, your *soul*. But he gave everything in return. And to have this part of Heathcliff was a rare and beautiful gift.

I lost myself in the sensations as we moved together, grinding against each other, lost in each other.

"Are you worried about being late for dinner now, gorgeous?" Morrie grinned against my earlobe as he ran his hands down my body, drawing out pleasure through my skin as Heathcliff filled me up.

"I think I *am* the dinner."

"You *are* the filling in a rather delectable villain sandwich," Morrie mused. "But what if I could make you come even faster? What if I could make you forget all about your fears?"

I knew exactly what he was asking. In response, I rolled my hips back. Morrie bit down my neck as he notched his body against mine. He'd already palmed some lube on his way over here. Of course he had. James Moriarty was like a filthy Boy Scout – always prepared for any eventuality.

Morrie's hand closed around my thigh, and his soft, commanding voice bid me to hold still. A drizzle of lube ran between my cheeks, followed by deft fingers, rubbing it in and around my hole.

"Do we have time?" Heathcliff quirked an eyebrow at him.

"I'll be quick." Morrie moved in behind me again, his hard cock dancing between my cheeks. "Trust me, after watching the two of you fuck like jackrabbits, I'll be so quick."

I gasped as he pushed his head inside. The stretch was so

intense, especially with Heathcliff's girth already buried deep. I felt myself tensing against him.

"Bite me, gorgeous," he purred, placing his hand over my mouth.

I bit down on his hand and gave myself a few moments of stillness to relax, then he pushed himself deeper. No matter how many times I did this with them – having one in each hole – it overwhelmed me in the best possible way.

"Our Mina," Morrie whispered against my ear as he thrust in another inch. "Such a filthy little minx."

I shivered beneath his words as he pushed inside me, deeper and deeper until he was completely sheathed.

Heathcliff's breath caught as he felt Morrie's cock pressing against him through my walls. No three people on earth could be closer than this. We were linked in body, mind, and soul.

Heathcliff growled, low and hungry. The darkness in his eyes seemed to spread across his whole body, bleeding into me, staking the hunger that burned inside me. He drew out slowly and thrust in deep, filling me.

And then it was Morrie's turn. He drew back just as Heathcliff pushed in, and his wicked laugh danced across my skin as he pumped his hips and buried himself inside me.

The pair of them were practiced at this now. They built a steady rhythm. I gripped the chair and Heathcliff's shoulders, giving myself over to them, trusting them to hold me and care for me. My pulse raced in my ears as my heart thudded in my chest.

Morrie's fingers dug into my hips. "That's it, gorgeous. Take us both deep. Good girl."

They fucked both holes, relentless and merciless. Sweat gleamed on Heathcliff's chest. Morrie's breath rushed past my ear. I was lost between them, a slave to the intense pleasure of sharing them with each other.

They're mine. And I'm theirs.

The thought gave me a burst of brightness, a power that

surged through my body and reminded me that I was Mina Wilde, I had done so much and come so far, and I had the love of three remarkable men. And no one, certainly not a bunch of writers, would take that away from me, no matter what they thought of me and my story.

I can do this.

Heathcliff's growls turned into a low moan. His lip curled as he came close to the edge. Morrie leaned over my shoulder and kissed him, digging his teeth into Heathcliff's lip, nipping him to give him the edge of pain that he knew Heathcliff loved.

With a cry smothered by Morrie's lips, Heathcliff came, his cock tightening inside me.

And I let go. I flew. I soared above myself and looked down at a woman with tangled hair and fire-laced eyes who was well-fucked and glistening and *vibrating* with pleasure and love. And when I came back, my body was warm and alive and more powerful than ever.

I rested against Heathcliff's broad chest, his cock still warm inside me, while Morrie gave a final pump and drew out, coming across my back.

This was an absolutely perfect moment. I wanted to stay here forever...

"What are you two doing?" Morrie mock-scolded us as he rose from his knees to resume his search for the perfect shirt. "You're laying about when we have less than an hour to get ready for dinner. Heathcliff, hang your clothes from the rafter so they don't dry with wrinkles in them! I thought you'd be showered already, Mina, especially since I'm going to have mine now."

"You're not having the first shower. You take forever, and I'm the guest of honor, not you!"

"Try and stop me, gorgeous." The bathroom door slammed shut.

"Say the word and I'll hang his testicles from the ceiling fan with piano wire," Heathcliff growled.

"I'm going to do it myself." I pulled myself reluctantly off Heathcliff, hobbled across the room, and rapped on the door. "James Moriarty, you give up that bathroom this instant, or I will tell Grimalkin where you hid your stash of imported French cheese…"

"You wouldn't!"

"I would!"

Okay, so maybe it's not perfect…

~

"How do you feel about meeting Hugh Briston now?" Morrie asked as he nudged his way past me in the bathroom so he could straighten his tie in the mirror.

I hurriedly brushed a bit of blusher on my cheeks. I'd been wearing a lot less makeup since my eyesight had worsened, not because I couldn't apply it – although it took a little longer now, or Quoth did it for me – but because I didn't notice other's people's makeup, so my own seemed less important. But I'd decided to go for a bit of makeup tonight. I wanted to make the right impression on Hugh and also to hide the 'just got fucked five ways from Sunday' glow in my cheeks.

"I'm excited. That really helped, thank you. I'm ready to get down there and pretend that I know what the hell I'm doing."

"You don't need to pretend, Mina." Heathcliff frowned as he ripped his trousers off the ironing board before Morrie could make a third attempt to iron out the wrinkles. "You deserve to be here."

I finished applying my lipstick and went back to the mess of clothing Morrie dumped on the bed, and started flinging it aside.

"What are you doing?" Heathcliff demanded. "I had everything arranged to match my room at home, and you've gone and messed it up."

"I packed a beaded clutch in one of the bags, but I can't

remember which one." I bent down to unzip Quoth's rucksack, and pulled out a small black leather toiletry bag. "If Heathcliff took it out to fit in that second bottle of Scotch or those twenty-five books, I will not be amused—"

"Whoa, gorgeous," Morrie stalked across the room on his long legs. He took the case from my hands and helped me to my feet. "Come away from there. You don't want to wrinkle your dress. Heathcliff and I will find the purse."

"Speak for yourself," Heathcliff muttered from his chair by the fireplace as he started the difficult work of re-wrinkling his trousers. I heard a page turn in his book.

"Fine. Oscar, come help!" Morrie called. Oscar leaped up from his doggie bed under the window. "If you could root through Heathcliff's bag while I look through my things, there's a good boy..."

"Fine, fine." Heathcliff stood up and shuffled over. He pulled something out from under the bed. "Is this it?"

"That's the one." I dropped my lipstick and ID inside. I glanced at my phone on the floor near Heathcliff's chair. My fingers itched to take it with me. *No, Heathcliff's right. I'm supposed to be on holiday.* I checked that the matching bandana I'd tied around Oscar's harness was straight. "Quoth's not here, though."

"You know what he's like in bird form," Heathcliff said. "Time doesn't move the same."

I looked toward the window, a flicker of sadness licking my heart that Quoth wouldn't be with us. But I knew he wouldn't be late without a good reason. He must've been enjoying talking to the ravens.

"We'll leave the window open a crack for him," Morrie said, dropping the spare room key on the window sill. "Does that work?"

"Yes." I sucked in a breath and smoothed my dress down one more time. "We can go now."

Heathcliff stared forlornly at his book, then checked his whisky flask was securely stashed in his pocket.

Morrie tucked the toiletries bag back into the bottom of Quoth's rucksack, smoothed down his impeccable suit, and offered me his other arm. "Let us wow them, gorgeous."

CHAPTER FIVE

*V*oices and tinkling piano music greeted us as we moved downstairs. My stomach squirmed with fresh nerves, but I stamped them down.

I'm Mina Wilde and I have put several murderers behind bars. I am dating three of the most famous villains from classic literature. I can walk into a room and talk to some writers.

We moved through the deserted main lobby and down a wide hallway to the music room. This was a large, high-ceilinged room behind the restaurant where Meddleworth held cocktail events and small concerts. According to Jonathan, it was once a drawing room where the guests at a banquet would retire for the evening to listen to the piano or play cards. My heels and Oscar's toes click-clacked across the marble floor. I could see it was a checkerboard pattern of black and white marble – that sort of contrast stood out to my eyes and made the room instantly more interesting.

"There are a variety of trays being passed around by the wait-staff," Morrie whispered to me, giving me a description of the dark corners of the room I couldn't quite see. "About thirty people are present, although none of them are as radiant as you. Someone is murdering a grand piano in the corner—"

"No murder," I whispered back. "This is a murder-free holiday, remember?"

"If you say so, gorgeous. There are leather couches arranged under the window, and to your left is the bar—"

"Ah, sweet, fortifying alcohol." Heathcliff slid his arm out from beneath my hand and bent over to kiss the top of my head. "I'll be right back."

He disappeared into the room before I could ask him to bring me back a gin and tonic. Morrie laughed. "Don't worry, gorgeous. I'll be by your side."

I made a dismissive gesture with my hand. "I'm not nervous. You cured me, remember?"

"Ah, but you forget that I know you. You've spent the last month stalking all these people on social media and learning every detail about them so you can make a good first impression," Morrie pointed out. "Getting some excellent sex isn't going to change that. I like to think you did that with me – if you google my name, you get all kinds of salacious fanfiction, most of which would be much closer to the truth of my life than Doyle's stuffy old novel."

"You've been googling yourself?" I asked.

"But of course."

"That's on-brand. Can we get—"

"Are you Mina Wilde?"

I turned toward the voice. The room is bright enough that I can make out the shape of a petite woman with wavy blonde hair wearing a stunning black sheath dress.

"I'm Mina." I thrust out my hand for her to shake.

Her hand closed over mine in a friendly, excitable shake. She shook Morrie's hand, too. "I'm Christina Olivian. I recognize your picture from your biography. It's so lovely to meet you. I've been enjoying your story. Very racy!"

"I've been enjoying yours, too." I recognized Christina's name from the stack of excerpts we had to read as part of our pre-retreat homework. Of all the other writers, Christina's story was my favorite. It was a haunting mystery of a missing girl and a Yorkshire manor house, told over three generations of women. It had a brooding, gothic vibe that captivated me, and I knew Heathcliff would love it.

But then, I wasn't surprised. I went googling, too. Christina was already an accomplished writer, with two books already published (albeit by small presses) to critical acclaim. In person, she sounded much younger than her literary achievements and her lush work made her seem.

"Thank you. I'm really hoping that everything I learn from Hugh will get my manuscript where it needs to be. I'm hoping it will be my breakout book. Is this your agent?" She turned toward Morrie.

"No. No agent. This is Morrie, one of my um…boyfriends." It was weird to have to say that to a stranger. Everyone in Argleton was so used to seeing me with Heathcliff, Morrie, and Quoth that no one batted an eyelid anymore. Even my mother had got on board with my unconventional relationship and admitted that having three strapping guys around to open pickle jars and remove spiders from the shower had its advantages. If people gossiped about us back in Argleton, they did it in the traditional British way – behind our backs.

When I received the invitation to the retreat and noticed all the meals included a +1, I'd gone back and forth about how I should approach my harem. But ultimately I'd decided that I had nothing to feel ashamed about, and so I'd emailed Meddleworth's owner and the retreat organizer, Donna Bollstead, and asked if all three of my boyfriends could be included in the group activities if we paid the extra. Donna was great about it.

Part of living in the world meant that people would ask questions about my relationship, especially if they read my book. But

I felt prepared for that. It was some of the other stuff I didn't know if I was ready for.

"Oh, how wonderful. Just like in your book!" Christina leaned in, whispering loudly, "I'm so curious about what it's like to be so open about dating three guys. Most men are far too jealous to consider such a thing, so we women usually have to be more secretive about it."

"Oh, well, I'm not sure that's the answer—"

"I'm here with my boyfriend, Killian Stafford. He's also my agent. He wouldn't want me to have another boyfriend at all. He'd kill any guy who laid a finger on me. He's such a jealous prick. What did you do to get your guys to agree? Aren't they jealous of each other? Do they fight over you?"

I tried to remember what I'd read in *The Ethical Slut*. "I guess we don't feel right being jealous when someone we love is happy—"

But Christina seemed to be one of those people who didn't need the other side of a conversation. "Killian's great, really he is. He's not a writer, but he's been *so* supportive of my career. He's going to sit in on the classes and make sure I get as much as possible out of them. I can't wait to learn from Hugh. I'll do *anything* to get to the next level—"

"That sounds an awful lot like a promise," a sour voice said from behind her. "Are you planning to stab your fellow writers in their sleep?"

Christina laughed off the comment as the sour man joined our group. "Don't mind him. This is Charlie Doyle. He's the police procedural writer of our little group. I think the two of you will get on splendidly, as Charlie also writes books set in a small English village—"

"If this is Mina Wilde with her amateur bookshop sleuth, our work is nothing alike," Charlie scoffed. "I'm an ex-cop with thirty-three years on the force, and I slaved over my manuscript for ten years, getting every factual detail absolutely perfect.

Whereas I could tell from the first chapter of Mina's book that the mystery is fraught with procedural errors. This is why policing – like writing – should be left to the professionals."

Morrie's fingers gripped my hand. "Mina is an excellent writer. I happen to be a connoisseur of murders, and I can tell you that she has got the details right in her book."

I managed to hold back my grin.

"With all due respect, sir, since you look like an educated man," Charlie punched the air with his finger for emphasis. He enjoyed having everyone's attention. "But how is a blind woman going to write a convincing book? How can she describe what she cannot see—argh!"

Charlie's tirade against me cut off with a yelp as he jerked away suddenly. A dark shadow moved in front of him, and I gathered from the frantic dance he was doing that someone had tipped a dram of whisky over his head.

"Oops," Heathcliff said drolly, placing his empty glass back on the bar. "I'm such a butterfingers."

"You clumsy oaf," Charlie roared. "Now I'm all sticky. I have scotch dripping into my shoes, and this is a *silk* tie—"

"Oh, here, let me help you with that." Morrie moved forward. I could have stopped him, but after Charlie's comments about my eyesight and his implication that my books, which were based on my life, were factually inaccurate, I didn't want to.

Morrie grabbed Charlie's tie, muttering about dry cleaning and fiber saturation points. A moment later, Charlie yelled again. Morrie stepped back to reveal orange flames leaping from Charlie's chest.

"My tie is on fire!" Charlie yelled, spinning wildly, his voice thick with panic. Everyone in the room scrambled to get away from him.

"Golly, it is too," Morrie said as he returned to my side. "I don't know how that happened."

"Croak!"

A dark shape blew through the door of the music room and dived straight at Charlie.

"Argh, a bird!" Charlie raised his hands to protect his face, completely forgetting that his tie was on fire. His sleeves caught fire, too. The smell of singed fabric scented the air, and a fire alarm wailed.

Charlie dropped to his stomach and started trying to roll the rug over him to put out the flames. The only problem was that the rug was weighed down by furniture and party guests. He whipped it out from beneath a woman's foot, and she toppled over into the arms of another man.

"You fool!" She kicked Charlie in the side. "Get off the floor and dunk your tie in the bathroom."

There was now a black spot on the rug where the fire had attacked it. I was struggling to hold in my laughter. Beside me, Morrie's whole body was trembling with mirth, and I could hear Heathcliff snort at the bar. I couldn't turn and face them or I'd lose it completely. Instead, I searched frantically for Quoth.

He was sitting on top of the curtain rail, and as soon as Charlie staggered to his feet, Quoth dive-bombed him.

You will never, ever say things like that about my Mina, ever again.

Quoth circled Charlie's head, lifted a leg, and let fly a giant poop. Years of honing his aim on annoying, poetry-reciting bookshop customers paid off, and Quoth's package landed straight into Charlie's face.

"Aarrrrrrrgh!" Charlie yelled.

I could no longer contain my laughter, but luckily, the rest of the room joined me. Rage radiated off Charlie as he wiped his fingers through the mess and stalked off, his shoes squelching with every step.

"I got you a drink." Heathcliff pressed a glass into my hand. I raised it to my lips. A G&T. My favorite. My heart flooded with love for my guys.

Morrie squeezed my hand. "If anyone else gives you trouble,

just you let us know."

"I will, I promise."

Quoth came down and settled on my shoulder. I patted his head affectionately. "That was brilliant, all of you. But seriously, I can handle a little criticism. I'm here to learn, after all. Not everyone has to like my books."

"But that guy said you couldn't write a book because you're blind," Christina piped up, smoothing down her dress as she rejoined our group. "He deserved everything he got."

"Croak." Quoth nodded his head vigorously in agreement.

"I can't believe that bird is just sitting on your shoulder like that. Aren't you afraid he has the bird flu or will peck your eyeball out?" Christina said.

"Not at all. Ravens are very intelligent. This one proved that." I patted Quoth's head and he nudged my hand, making a little *nyuh-nyuh-nyuh* sound as one of the trays passed by. I swiped a salmon puff off it and held it up to Quoth, who gobbled it hungrily.

I'm sorry I was late, Mina. I was talking to the ravens and...well, there's something I might need some help with—

"If you'll excuse me, ma'am." Jonathan appeared by my side in a flash. He wrapped his huge hands gently around Quoth. "I'm terribly sorry if this bird distressed you. The little blighter must've run inside when I came in from getting the car. I'll put him back with the others, and he won't disturb ye again."

"It's fine, Jonathan." I patted Quoth's head again. "He fought for my honor. I think he's a rather lovely little bird."

You'd better remember that later, Quoth warned. *I saw through the window what you got up to with Morrie and Heathcliff, and I have plans of my own.*

A delicious shiver ran down my spine. I gripped Oscar's harness tighter. Morrie plucked a tiny meatball off a nearby tray and fed it to Quoth.

"Has your friend shown up yet?" Jonathan asked as he allowed

Quoth to finish the meatball before tucking him securely into his shoulder. "I haven't seen him, but I've been busy dealing with your car. I've pulled most of the larger pieces out and left them in the staff car park around the back, next to my range rover. There's a workshop there. Our metalworking tutor, Melinda, will take a look and see if she can fix it, but I think the car is a goner."

"Our friend Allan arrived a little while ago," I said. "He's up in our room having a rest, but he'll be joining us for dinner shortly, won't he? Especially since I left the window in our suite open a crack."

Thank you, Mina. You think of everything.

"That's not a good idea." Jonathan frowned. "The weather is going to get worse tonight, and we should have a full-on storm tomorrow. The rain will come in sideways with the wind and ruin all your things. I'll go and close it for you—"

"No!" I cried louder than I intended. I lowered my voice. "I mean, Allan will close it when he comes down. He just...likes the fresh, crisp country air."

"Very well, ma'am." Jonathan nodded to the rest of our group. "I'd best be off and leave you to your drinks. I have to put this wee fella back with his family."

See you soon, Mina. See if you can save some more of those meatballs for me. When you get a spare moment, I'll tell you about the ravens.

"Well, that was certainly an adventure." Christina grabbed two glasses of bubbles off a tray and handed one to me. I shook my head, still nursing my G&T. Heathcliff leaned across me, swiping for the bubbly, but someone else got there first.

"Thanks for that, old girl." A posh-sounding man plucked the glass of bubbly from Christina's hand and turned to Morrie. "I must say, I don't know how you chaps did that, but setting that foul old policeman's tie on fire was quite the sport."

"I had nothing to do with it," Morrie said in his sweetest, most innocent voice.

"Yes, yes, I understand. You must keep mum. Plausible deniability and whatnot. Even so, good show. I don't even know why Charlie bothered to show up at this retreat. Hugh won't be choosing his gritty little police stories when there is real work of substance like my Christina's." He flashed a smile so bright even I could see it. "And yours, of course, sir."

"Oh, I'm not a crime writer," Morrie waved a hand dismissively. "At least, the kind of crime writing I do is detailed plans on how to commit them. I'm here with Mina."

"Oh. Right. Yes, of course." The guy's gaze flicked to me for a moment before moving quickly away.

Christina frowned. "This is my partner, Killian. I'm sorry, Mina, that he's a sexist pig and assumed that only men can write crime fiction."

"Killian Stafford, literary agent." Killian extended a hand. I didn't want to shake it but I thought that might be too much of a snub. "I'm hoping that once Christina has wowed Hugh with her work, I can swoop in and seal the deal."

"You sound confident," Morrie said. "But any one of the retreat writers could end up with the publishing contract."

"Our deal is as good as done, I'm afraid." Killian puffed out his chest. "I've already connected Christina with Hugh on numerous occasions. He's said that he wants Christina at Red Herring Press, but it's just a matter of her writing the perfect book. And we think her new manuscript is the one. Hugh and I just have a few clauses to iron out and we're ready to seal the deal."

"Then what are the rest of us doing here?" I asked, my chest tightening. The advertisement for the retreat said that Hugh chose one writer every year to champion through his company. If Christina was that author, did that mean I didn't even have a chance?

"I know what I'm doing here," a woman leaned into our circle and whispered conspiratorially. "I'm here to make sure Hugh Briston *pays*."

CHAPTER SIX

"*I*f our friend Charlie were here, he'd say that sounded like a threat," Morrie said.

"Oh, it is a threat." The woman laughed, her throaty voice cutting the air with tension. "I want to watch that foul man dance on the end of his own noose."

I opened my mouth to say something, but realized I had no response. What do you even say to that?

Relax, Mina – people make idle threats all the time. Just because you're used to seeing murder everywhere, doesn't mean that this woman actually intends to do Hugh Briston harm.

Beside me, Killian guffawed. "I'm surprised Hugh let you in, Vivianne. Isn't there a restraining order?"

"That was a rumor Hugh put around to make me seem like a hysterical woman. But that's where I'm clever." Vivianne lifted a finger. My eyes caught the glint of several sparkling jewels on her fingers. "I'm here under a pseudonym. Helena Fox. I'm going to make my ex-husband's weekend as miserable as he made the last fifteen years of my life."

"Sounds like a good plan to me," Heathcliff said. "I'm big on revenge, myself. Maybe we can swap tips?"

But Vivianne wasn't listening. She leaned forward into our circle, her voice dripping with venom as she continued her story. "For fifteen years I followed that man all over the world while he built the Red Herring empire. I smiled for his publishing friends and let literary agents fondle me beneath the table if it would land him the deal he wanted. I did everything for that man, and how did he repay me?" Her voice rose above the din. "He repaid me by divorcing me when I got 'past my prime,' and cutting me off without a cent. Well, I'll have the final laugh. Just you wait. You all have a ringside seat for the literary drama of the decade."

With those final damming words, she spun on her heel and stomped off. I heard another woman cry out as Vivianne nearly bowled her over.

"Don't go running off now." The new woman clapped her hands, and the room fell silent. "Hello, writers and your guests. My name is Donna Bollstead, the owner of Meddleworth House. I've recently inherited Meddleworth from my parents, who tragically died in a boating accident in the summer. Those of you who've attended literary events at Meddleworth before may notice some changes around here, namely the opening of our brand-new spa and wellness center. The castle – like the changing landscape of the book world – must move with the times, but I think you'll see that we're just as dedicated to preserving Meddleworth's literary heritage as ever."

"Please," Killian scoffed at us as he raised his glass. "Donna would sell every first edition in the library if she could make more room for her precious spa."

Christina shushed him.

"Donna sounds young," I whispered to Morrie.

"She looks about your age," he whispered back. "Though her breasts aren't nearly as—"

"Too much information, thanks." I turned back to listen to what Donna is saying.

"—Hugh's flight in from New York City was held up by the

bad weather, but he's just in his room freshening up and will be down here any moment. Please enjoy the free drinks, canapés, and entertainment, and we will retire to the restaurant at 7PM for a seated dinner. Thank you."

"Enjoy I shall." Heathcliff whirled around and headed back to the bar, leaving us with Killian and Christina. I leaned down and nervously touched the bandana I'd tied to Oscar's harness. It was covered in cute cartoon skulls, and the color perfectly matched my dress. Just knowing Oscar was at my feet and Morrie was at my side made my nerves a little calmer.

Hugh will be here any minute...

"This is a pretty nice party Donna's put on for us," I said to Christina.

"It's all so much more opulent than I remember," Christina said. "I must say, I prefer Champagne and canapés to the beer and crackers they had last time."

"You've been here before?"

"I attended the retreat three years ago when Donna's parents still ran the hotel. There was no spa, the rooms weren't nearly as lush, and the restaurant was more of a pub. I like what Donna's done with the place. I feel like I'm going to write some amazing words here."

"With the price tag on this retreat, you'd better," Killian muttered. "Donna's making a killing from us this week. But it will all be worth it when Hugh publishes Christina's book."

I decided not to rise to his bait. I got the feeling that Killian made his money from his confidence, and I knew from wrangling Morrie's ego that just because a guy like Killian said the deal was done didn't mean the ink was dry yet.

But he was right about the price tag. As an author accepted for the retreat, I receive a stipend toward my travel costs, but I still had to pay for my room and the retreat fee, not to mention for all the guys to stay, too. Morrie offered to pay the bill for us, but even his eyes popped out when he saw the final figures. I'd heard the retreat used to be different, a lot more casual, but I'd also heard it was a bit of a boys' club, and I was happy they were at least trying to be more inclusive, even if the cost would prevent some writers from attending.

"Who are all these other people in the room?" I asked Christina, who had definitely shown herself to be the friendliest of the writers. "It sounds like there are forty or fifty people here."

"Oh, they're special invited guests of Donna's. Most of them are other writers or publishing industry folk, or previous retreat graduates. Donna's parents were both writers, and they used Meddleworth as a bit of a literary salon, which between you and me is not a path to riches. When I was here last it was clear the place was falling apart, but they didn't seem to care as long as they were surrounded by writers creating things. After their tragic deaths, Donna took over the castle, and she's been trying to make the place profitable with the spa and the classes." Christina swept her arm around the room. "Would you believe that all these people have been badmouthing her for months, talking about how she's stomping on her parents' legacies? But they'll all show up for the free Champagne and canapés."

"Ah. I get it." I smiled as I thought about the way some people acted after I started making changes at Nevermore. "That sort of thing rubs the literary snobs the wrong way. I get a little of that at my bookshop. People complain that the popular genre fiction gets pride of place in the displays over such vital classics like Dickens and Tolstoy and the Brontë sisters, but the truth is that we have to put out what sells. People should be able to read what they like, no judgments given. And if we don't make money, another independent bookshop dies."

"Exactly." Christina grinned. "Hey, can I do a signing in your shop, maybe? I want to support independent bookshops."

"I'll take care of the details." Killian shoved his way in front of her and leered over me, obviously sensing the chance to make a deal. "When her new book comes out with Red Herring Press, it's going to be a huge smash. You'll need to order at least a thousand copies, but I'm sure you'll sell out—"

"He's here!" someone behind us whispered.

"About time," another man grumbled. "I don't think I can stay in this stuffy, stodgy room another minute. Could you pass me another bubbly? These are all free, aren't they?"

"The man himself arrives." Killian nudged Christina. "Come on, my beautiful prize. Let us get you some face time with our soon-to-be golden ticket."

That's such a weird way to talk about your girlfriend.

"Ooooh!" Christina drifted away without even saying good-bye. A moment later I heard her blowing air kisses to someone near the doorway. "Hugh, darling. It's so good to see you again."

"The eagle has landed," Morrie whispered.

He didn't have to tell me. There was a flutter in the air as everyone in the room gravitated toward an imposing figure who appeared at Donna's side beneath the enormous double doors. I shifted my weight between my feet, suddenly nervous. Over there was a man who could make my dreams come true. I'd already had one career crushed by discrimination. I *needed* this to work.

"Are you going to talk to him?"

"I…" I struggled to find the words. "I don't want to push my way through everyone and be just another face in the crowd. I don't think you should bombard someone before they've even made it to the bar. Perhaps I'll…I'll go to the bathroom."

"Bwack bwack bwack." Morrie did a chicken dance.

"Shhhhh." I swatted his hand. "I'll talk to him later. I promise."

I directed Oscar down a long corridor toward the bathrooms. There were two bathroom stalls and then a separate disabled bathroom. I pulled Oscar into the disabled bathroom, did my business, washed my hands, and then reached into my purse for my lipstick, trying to force the butterflies flapping around my stomach back into their cage.

"You've got this, Mina," I reminded myself. "You are the daughter of one of the most famous poets of all time. You have literally slayed a centuries-old vampire who came from a horror novel. You can go out there and talk to a man about a book."

But first, I'll just do a little touch-up. Then I'll walk out there and wow Hugh Briston's socks off.

I reapplied my lipstick, checked that my hair wasn't drooping, and was replacing the lipstick in my purse when Oscar let out a whine.

"What's the matter, boy?"

I turned to the locked bathroom door just as something heavy pounded against it. My heart leaped into my throat. The heavy wooden door groaned as it was battered from the other side.

It sounded like someone was trying to break the door down!

CHAPTER SEVEN

"What...what's going on?" I called out, my breath catching. "This bathroom is occupied."

"Awwwwwwwwwwoooooooo," a voice called back. My heart hammered against my ribs. The thumping and banging continued. Oscar scrambled over and pawed at the door. I didn't want him anywhere near it, because it sounded like the door might give way at any moment. I grabbed Oscar's harness and yanked him back, making him sit by my side as I frantically tried to figure out what to do next.

I know, I'll call Heathcliff. He'll scare the brute away.

I pulled out my phone and had just commanded it to dial Heathcliff when I heard another voice outside the door, faint and muffled through the thick wood and the even thicker castle walls.

"Argh, Fergus, you get back, you old beast."

I recognized Jonathan's voice. He grunted and huffed for a bit, and then called out, "If anyone's in there, it's safe for ye to come out. I've got hold of him."

Tentatively, I reached forward and pulled the door open. Oscar barked with happiness and dragged me outside.

Jonathan stood in the hallway, holding back an enormous, excitable dog with a black and white coat who was frantically trying to break away to lick me to death. Oscar stayed with me, as he was trained to do, but I could tell from the way that he pulled on the harness that he wanted to meet his new friend.

"I'm sorry, love." Jonathan grappled with the dog's lead. "This is Fergus. He usually stays in the staff quarters while I'm on duty, but he escaped while my back was turned. I bet he frightened ye something terrible!"

"A little bit." I smiled at the dog as he slobbered excitedly all over Jonathan's hand. He was at least twice the size of Oscar and made purely of muscle, with an enormous head and a mouth filled with sharp teeth, but up close it was clear Fergus was a giant teddy bear. I realized that the bangs and thumps I'd heard were Fergus throwing himself against the wooden door to try and get inside. "I think he wanted to make friends with Oscar."

"Aye. He's an Irish wolfhound, great to have with me while I'm working on the estate. Fergus and I've been together since he was a wee pup." Jonathan patted Fergus' head affectionately. "He didn't mean to do that to the door – he always wants to be in the room where I am, and he probably smelled your Oscar and wanted to play. He thinks that if he throws himself against the door, he'll be able to break it down and get inside."

"I think he may be right," I laughed. "And it's fine. I'm familiar with this behavior. I'll often hear Oscar's paws scrabbling at a locked door if he thinks I'm somewhere having fun without him."

We brought the dogs together and let them sniff and lick each other. Fergus was so happy to make a new friend that he wound his lead around Jonathan's legs and nearly tripped him up.

Jonathan untangled himself. "I'll best be getting Fergus back to his room and locking him in with a pig's ear for the night. If Donna catches him in here where the guests are, we'll both be out on our arses, won't we, boy?"

"Woof!" Fergus declared.

"Arf," Oscar agreed.

"If Oscar wants some exercise while you're here, you're welcome to walk with me and Fergus on our morning rounds," Jonathan said. "Or, I'm happy to walk him for you while you're at the retreat. There's plenty on the grounds for him to enjoy."

"I may just take you up on that." I touched my hair, which thankfully had survived my terrifying bathroom encounter. "I'd better get back out there. The famous Hugh has arrived."

"Aye, that he has. Holding court out there like he's God's gift," Jonathan muttered.

"You're not the biggest Hugh Briston fan?" I asked.

"Aye, but that's only an old codger talking. Never you mind me," Jonathan patted Fergus' head. "Hugh's been coming to the castle for years to hold his retreats. The Bollsteads adored him, but he's got no respect for the history of this place. This castle and the grounds are so beautiful. They've been my home for my entire life, and I don't like to see people take advantage of them. You're a sweet girl, Mina. Watch yourself around Hugh, that's all I have to say about that."

Jonathan started dragging an excited Fergus down the hallway. As I followed them back toward the music room, Heathcliff, Morrie, and a freshly showered and dressed Quoth raced around the corner, nearly skidding into us.

"What happened?" Heathcliff demanded, waving his phone about. "This infernal device sent me an SOS message."

"We thought Charlie might have come back to get his revenge." Morrie's words were casual, but his voice trembled with panic.

I laughed. "Thank you all for coming to my rescue. Oscar and I were trapped in the bathroom by Fergus here, but it turns out that he just wanted some new friends."

"Oooh, he does want some friends, doesn't he?" Heathcliff

dropped to his knee to rub Fergus' ears. The dog whined with happiness and nuzzled into Heathcliff, who was getting dog hair all over his suit but didn't care.

My heart did that flip-flop thing it does whenever grumpy, growly Heathcliff went all gooey over an animal. We all had to take turns petting Fergus before Jonathan hurried him away. Morrie had to grab Heathcliff's arm to stop him from going after Fergus.

"Not so fast, big guy. You're needed here. Mina's got to get back out there and speak to Hugh, and judging by the level of crazy we've already seen tonight, she needs protection."

"She doesn't need protection. She just needs to stop being cornered by crazy writers and adorable doggos so she can work up the courage to walk up to the guy and introduce herself—"

"Um, guys," Quoth piped up, his voice nervous. "Mina might get her chance sooner than you think. Hugh Briston's walking down the hallway toward us now."

I whirled around, and could just make out a dark figure striding purposefully down the long, narrow hallway toward the restrooms. I immediately flattened myself against the wall.

"I can't harass him on the way to the bathroom!"

"We're completely blocking his path," Morrie pointed out. "Not saying anything is even weirder. Go."

Morrie gave me a gentle shove toward the hallway, and Oscar trotted off in that direction. *I guess I'm doing this.*

As I got nearer to Hugh, I could make out a few details about him. I'd had Quoth describe his picture to me before we came, so I knew he had dark hair that he had cut short and neat, and a small goatee. He wore a dark suit that looked well-tailored from the silhouette. He wasn't quite as tall as Morrie or as broad as Heathcliff, but he was definitely imposing. We'd have to squash to get past each other.

"Hello, Mr. Briston." I extended my hand as he tried to scoot past me. "I'm Mina Wilde. I'm one of the students in the retreat. I just wanted to say thank you so much for having me on the course. I'm really looking forward to hearing your thoughts on my work and—"

"I'll tell you my thoughts right now, Mina," Hugh snapped. "You don't belong here."

CHAPTER EIGHT

"*E*xcuse me?"

My heart hammered against my chest.

He didn't just say that, did he? I must have heard him wrong. My nerves are getting the better of me—

"I must admit to being intrigued by your application," Hugh continued. "The real-life amateur sleuth writing an amateur-sleuth tale. But when I read your sample pages I knew I was looking at someone who didn't understand the first thing about literary devices."

Oscar growled as Hugh tried to step past him. Oscar almost never growled. I bent down to try and calm him.

Hugh sniffed. "Your idea of literary fictional characters coming to life and meddling with modern affairs could have been a clever satire on our obsession with venerating certain works of classical literature without criticism, but you are not clever enough to pull it off. What I read was a lumpy pudding of a book – a teenage girl's erotic dream wrapped up in the trappings of a novel. The mystery is simplistic, the romance distracting, the sex gratuitous and absurd, and the whole thing a genre mishmash that no one asked for."

I reeled from the harshness of his words. My eyes pricked with tears. My book was a thinly-veiled fictionalized account of my life in the bookshop with the guys. It detailed how I solved the murder of Ashley Greer, my ex-best friend, and the beautiful and confusing time when I returned to Argleton and fell in love with three fictional villains.

Hugh Briston wasn't just calling my novel rubbish – he was taking aim at my *life*.

I gasped for air. It felt like he'd driven his fist into my gut.

"I…I'm sorry you feel this way," I managed to blurt out, glancing back at the guys in the desperate hope that they'd come and light Hugh Briston on fire. But they were trying to give me space to impress him. I couldn't count on them to always sweep in and save me. I swallowed back my tears and tried again. "You must see some potential, or I wouldn't be at the retreat…"

"Truthfully, the publishers told me that if I want to continue as editor, I have to be more *inclusive* of different styles and ideas. I have to stop only publishing books by old, white men, as if that's the criteria I use to choose my authors! I pick the best stories by the best writers, and if they all happen to look the same, that's not my problem. Two of my authors last year were women. But apparently, out of one hundred-and-eighty books on my list, that's not *enough*. It's all a load of PC, namby-pamby bollocks, if you ask me. But that's the world today. So here we are – you have your place on my retreat and I'm stuck reading a manuscript that's as ridiculous and confusing as a llama loose in Marks and Spencer."

Don't cry don't cry don't cry…

"So I should just…go home?"

"What, and tell the media that mean old Hugh Briston kicked out the blind girl?" he scoffed. "Not your wisest choice. You'll send the sharks after me, which would be an annoyance, but nothing I haven't handled before. Meanwhile, you will have burned every bridge in this industry. No publisher would touch you after you come after me. You paid the fee to be here, so I suppose you can attend the workshops and group critiques. Perhaps you will learn how real writers do it. Or you might prefer to spend the week in the spa, having the cotton wool between your ears plumped and steamed." Hugh waved a hand dismissively.

"I'll see you in tomorrow's workshop," I said through gritted teeth. If he thought he could get rid of me that easily, he hadn't met Mina Wilde.

"As you wish. But do not think for a moment that Red Herring would be interested in publishing this mess of a bodice ripper masquerading as a mystery. It's good for an internet chat-room for lonely spinsters, and nothing more. Good evening."

With that, Hugh elbowed his way past me and disappeared into the men's loo.

I slumped against the wall, too stunned and hurt to hold myself upright any longer. Hugh's insults circled over and over in my head. He hated my book. He hated everything about it – the mystery, the romance…

I can't do anything right.

Maybe I don't have what it takes to be a writer.

"Mina?" A voice called me back from my dark thoughts. I blinked, and my vision swam as tears welled in my eyes. Warm arms went around me. Quoth. Of course it was Quoth. "Are you okay? You're shaking. What did Hugh say to you?"

"He said…" I sniffed. "He said that he hates my book. He hates everything about it. He said that he only accepted me on the retreat because I'm ticking a diversity box for his publisher. He said that I shouldn't even bother attending the workshops…"

"I'll kill him," Heathcliff growled, appearing behind Quoth.

"No." I grabbed Heathcliff's arm. "You can't do that."

"He insulted you," Morrie said. "He deserves to die for that."

"Far be it for me to agree with Count Crotchety and the Charlemagne of Crime." Quoth's soft lips kissed away the tears beneath my eyes before they could fall. "But if he said all that to you, I will peck his eyes out and eat them in front of him."

"I'm the *Napoleon* of Crime, and you know it, birdie." Morrie elbowed Quoth in the ribs. "And that gibface flapdoodle is wrong about you, gorgeous. Your book is excellent. It's a fun story and you tell it well."

"Gibface flapdoodle?" I wheezed, clutching my stomach as a barking laugh burst out of me. Trust the three of them to find a way to make me laugh.

"Heathcliff told me that one. It's from his book of Shakespearean insults. If you prefer, I could mention that if his brain was made of dynamite, there wouldn't be enough to blow his hat off. Although," he rubbed his chin. "Perhaps I could help with that..."

"No dynamite," I sniffed, but I couldn't help the tiny smile tugging on my lips.

"His family tree must look like a cactus," Heathcliff added, seemingly catching onto the game. "Because everyone on it is a giant prick."

Quoth piped up. "He's the reason that the gene pool needs a lifeguard."

Tears of laughter streamed down my cheeks. I knew I was ruining my makeup, but did it even matter now? I'd been trying to impress Hugh Briston, but that ship hadn't just sailed, it had been ravaged by pirates.

Morrie struck a pose like an orator. His recent season starring in the Argleton Shakespeare festival as Macbeth had definitely rubbed off on him. "Just because Briston's a literary snob and his birth certificate is an apology letter to the condom factory, doesn't mean—"

"It's not that..." My mind whirred through Hugh's criticism. "I guess my book *is* a mashup of genres. And maybe I made the romance too much of a focus? People can be pretty derisive of romance, which is ridiculous, but it is a big part of the plot. And the heroine has three lovers – maybe that's too odd for mainstream literature..."

"Who's calling us odd?" Heathcliff cracks his knuckles. "I'll harvest his toes."

"I'd like to curse him so that every time he puts on socks, one of them is always slightly rotated, just enough to be uncomfortable," Quoth said with a perfectly deadpan voice. It took me several moments to stop laughing enough to be able to speak.

"It's fine. I guess that...I forget sometimes that what we have is unusual. It's not for everyone." I fold my arms, making my decision. "There's an audience out there for our story, I know it, no matter what Hugh Briston says. He might be the most important voice in publishing, but he's not the only voice. I'm not going to let him get to me. I'll enjoy the retreat, learn as much as I can, and go home and make my story even better."

"Are you sure?" Morrie asked. "Because I think it would be fun to harvest his toes. Or, I have some rather imaginative ways of separating his—"

"I'm *sure.*" I plastered a smile on my face before Morrie could supply me with more grisly revenge fantasies. (Where did he even get 'harvesting toes' from?) I gripped Oscar's harness and gestured in the direction of the music room. "Now, can we go back to the party? I fully intend to drink all the gin and chase down the men with the trays and make sure there's not a single lamb kofta left for Briston."

"Alcohol won't solve all your problems." Morrie held out his arm and I slipped my hand beneath his. Quoth stood at my other arm, his hand resting protectively on the small of my back, pooling warmth across my skin.

"Neither does milk," Heathcliff snapped back as he stomped in front of us. "And the government still suggests we drink two glasses a day. Now, how much money do you think I'd have to pay the pianist in the corner to have her play Chopsticks on repeat all evening? If we're pulling Briston's beard out through his ear canal, I at least want to bespoil his eardrums."

CHAPTER NINE

Bree: I finally found Grimalkin asleep in the toy trunk in the children's room. I set her up in front of the fire in the flat, but she doesn't want to eat. She just lies there, staring into the flames.

I think she might have caught a rabbit or something and she's digesting it like a snake.

Oh, and Pax stabbed a first edition of Asterix the Gaul because Edward told him that the Italians were the bad guys. I'll replace it.

woke to the sounds of someone shuffling around our bedroom. I opened my eyes to find it still dark. Heathcliff snored beside me, his head denting my pillow and his thick arm draped over my middle. On the other side of him, Morrie spooned him, his cheek resting on Heathcliff's shoulder. My mind whirred, remembering that I was in a strange castle and I hadn't put my laptop and jewelry in the safe because Morrie insisted that he needed all the space inside for his collection of designer watches.

I bolted upright, grabbing the knife Heathcliff always slipped beneath his pillow and thrusting it at the dark gloom in front of me.

"Who's there? I may be blind but I once stabbed a vampire with a sword, so don't mess with me."

A dark shape moved across the window. "Mina?"

It was Quoth. I sagged with relief.

"I'm sorry I scared you." Quoth bent over and kissed the top of my head. "I was trying to be quiet."

"What are you doing?"

"Ssssh, go back to sleep." Quoth ran a hand through his long hair. "I'm hunting for my boots. Heathcliff dumped a whole pile of clothes on top of my things and I can't find anything."

"Why do you need your boots?"

"Oh, I...um...I thought that I'd get up before the whole castle and...and..."

"And go and talk to the ravens?" I knew how excited Quoth got every time he met his fellow birds. We didn't have ravens in the village, and we'd seen a few in London, but we'd always been too distracted by solving murders to stop and visit with them. In many ways, Quoth had always been more comfortable in himself when he was a raven, so it was nice for him to get to know other birds. And I remembered that he had something he wanted to tell me, but after meeting Hugh last night I wasn't much in the mood for conversation. I wrapped my arms around him and pulled him in close to me, breathing in his earthy, chocolatey scent. "Do you want me to come with you? We can talk about that thing you wanted to tell me yesterday."

Quoth's breath quickened. "That would be amazing. It will be easier to show you than to explain."

With my arms still around him, Quoth transformed into his raven. There was this beautiful moment as he shifted where the black feathers poked through his skin and he was still mostly human but coated in the smoothest, silky feathers. I loved to touch him as he shifted – he liked the reassurance of my presence and I liked to feel his bones breaking and reshaping into a whole new creature who was still completely, intrinsically Quoth.

He was remarkable because he was so impossible. But Quoth was real. He was here. And he was *mine*.

Quoth perched on top of the safe. I felt his fire-rimmed eyes follow me around the room as I pulled on jeans, a Patti Smith t-shirt, and a hoodie. I grabbed the room key and stirred Oscar awake, placing his harness in front of him and directing him to step into it. The three of us made our way downstairs, with Oscar trotting happily toward the main doors, excited to relieve himself and head out on a walk. Quoth hopped along on the floor behind us, carrying something under his wing and occasionally letting out a croak of excitement.

I threw open the heavy wooden front door of the hotel, and the cold air blasted my face. It wasn't raining, but the promise of a downpour clung to the frigid air. The clouds overhead were grey and low. I thought of Morrie's exploded car and reminded myself that we were trapped here, and at least the castle was warm and dry.

"Croak," Quoth called, hurrying in front of us as we made our way across the lawn, stopping near an overgrown fountain so Oscar could relieve himself. When he was done, Quoth led us across the lawn toward the aviary.

Oscar navigated around the worst of the puddles. He must remember that I yelled at him yesterday.

Mina, look! Quoth's voice landed inside my head. Our telepathic connection hummed with his excitement and...and distress. Quoth was anxious and upset, and I was about to find out why.

Oscar stopped at a long, mesh fence. It was too dim on the other side for me to make out anything except the dark shapes of trees and perches, but I could hear the voices of ravens croaking in greeting. Quoth walked tentatively up to the fence. He dropped his object through the window. I recognized it as one of Morrie's watches from his hoard in the safe.

"Quoth, did you take Morrie's watch from the safe?"

He won't miss it.

"I'm sorry – have you *met* Morrie?"

They'll enjoy it much more than he will, trust me.

I could hear the ravens prising off the back of the watch and breaking the links apart. I caught the flash of light as the first rays of sunlight peeking over the horizon picked up the glittering metal and row of diamonds around the bezel.

They say that my gift is acceptable, Quoth tells me. *I can be their friend.*

"Morrie will be pleased to hear it when he's late for his seaweed wrap because some ravens ate his Rolex," I murmured.

While Quoth swooped up to chatter to his new friends, Oscar and I walked along the length of the mesh fence, Quoth hopping along on top of it, talking in raven language to the birds inside. His thoughts in my head became a jumble of English and a language I didn't understand.

Only when we made our way back to where we began did I realize that we weren't at a fence at all, but on the outside of a large aviary. And the birds inside were growing agitated. I staggered back as one of them threw its body against the mesh.

"What's the matter with them?" I asked.

They want me to set them free, he told me. *They don't like being trapped in the aviary. They said that they used to be allowed to roam the estate freely, but since Donna took over, she didn't want them pooping on guests so she had Jonathan lock them away.*

"To be fair, that is a real problem." I grinned at Quoth, remembering all the times he'd left a 'surprise' on the heads of people who quoted 'The Raven' by Edgar Allen Poe. "It seems like a pretty big space for them…"

I trailed off as I thought about Quoth being trapped behind a mesh fence. I did not like that thought.

And I remembered Jonathan grabbing him last night and mentioning putting him back 'with the others.' Quoth *could* have been trapped in this cage if he hadn't escaped.

I didn't like that at all.

They can't fly more than six feet in the air. They can't soar. Their wings get ragged from hitting the fence all the time. They don't get to hunt unless an unfortunate mouse wanders into the cage. Did you know that a group of ravens is called an unkindness?

"That seems a bit mean," I say. "All the ravens I know are perfectly lovely."

What's unkind is keeping them trapped here like this. Quoth landed on my shoulder. The rising sun caught the glimmer of righteous fire in his irises. *Can we help them?*

"I don't think there's anything we can do. We're guests at the castle. We can't just go around letting the wildlife roam free. And besides, I wouldn't even know how we could do that. This fence must be pretty strong and the lock pretty secure if it can withstand ravens tampering with it."

They said that Jonathan installed a combination lock at first, but they figured out the combination and set themselves free. So Donna's installed a new electronic lock system that's supposed to be raven-proof. Mina, they're crying. They're not made for being in cages.

Quoth's words rang with passion and quiet anger. I remembered the art exhibit he created back in Argleton – the one that got destroyed when he tried to suck my blood after Dracula made him into his vampire servant. (I've had quite the year. Maybe one day I'll even write a book about it.) Quoth created an installation of bird cages, some with doors open, some with objects trapped inside. Walking through that exhibit was a glimpse inside his heart.

Quoth often felt trapped – not because we kept him in a cage, but because he didn't fit anywhere. Through our relationship, he'd been able to explore his emotions through art, go to school, exhibit his paintings, and have a future. He felt free, and he wanted to give these ravens the same feeling.

I bent down and touched Oscar's head. In many ways, I felt the same. When I first found out about my retinitis pigmentosa diagnosis, I felt trapped by it. But Nevermore Bookshop, and the guys, and Oscar, had made me see that my eyes weren't a curse that destroyed my life, but just another part of me.

I sighed. "I can't promise anything, but we can talk to Jonathan. Maybe he will be able to push back against Donna so they can be free."

Thank you, Mina. It means the world to them. And to me.

Quoth hopped along the top of the fence, croaking and making the nyuh-nyuh-nyuh voice in his throat as he chatted with the ravens inside. I gripped Oscar's lead tighter as fat raindrops started to fall on my shoulders. Oscar pulled on his lead. He wanted to keep walking, but I didn't want to wander around on my own in the wet.

"I'm going to head back in," I called to Quoth. "Did you want to come with me?"

I think I'll stay for a bit longer, if that's okay? I'll come back before I head off to my painting class.

"Of course." I waved goodbye to Quoth and directed Oscar back toward the path.

As we hurried toward the castle, I noticed a covered walkway leading around the side of the restaurant. That would keep us much drier than going back through the main entrance, especially if it led all the way around to the backdoor by the music room. I directed Oscar onto the walkway, and he got us underneath just as the rain started to really bucket down. It hammered against the roof above our heads as we hurried around the side of the castle.

As we rounded the corner of the restaurant, I overheard male voices. *Who would be outside in this weather? If it's Jonathan, maybe I can ask him about the ravens...*

But it wasn't Jonathan. I recognized Charlie Doyle and Hugh Briston. Before I even knew what I was doing, I flattened myself and Oscar against the house. Both of the men had been so horrible to me, I didn't want them to see me out here, alone, without any of the guys. I hoped they would finish their conversation and leave. I pulled the hood of my hoodie tight around my face to keep off the worst of the water.

Thankfully, the rain eased off a little, and I caught part of their conversation.

"—so it's all settled, then?" Charlie was saying. "You're sending the contract in the mail?"

"Just as soon as Red Herring's lawyers have drawn it up," Hugh said. "An ex-detective turned crime writer is going to be a big hit with our readers. It lends an air of authenticity to the books that the reading public eats up. The ghostwriter will contact you in a couple of weeks to—"

"Ghostwriter?" Charlie sounded petulant. "You never said anything about a ghostwriter. What about my book? I've been working on that manuscript for *years*."

"Yes, and it shows," Hugh snapped. "Your book is a steaming pile of crap written by someone who doesn't know how to write. But that's okay. The book doesn't matter – the package does. The star quality. I can make you a literary star, Charlie, and we both make truckloads of money. Leave the book to me – I've got a bunch of hacks on my payroll who will whip it into shape for primetime. They're mostly women, all young and hungry. I'll send you an attractive one. Do you prefer a blonde or redhead?"

I didn't think Hugh could be any worse, but yup, there it is.

"Could she be a blonde, like that Christina?" Charlie's voice rose hopefully.

Gross, gross, gross.

"If you like Christina, I'll assign her to you. Christina's coming to work as a ghostwriter shortly, just as soon as I can convince that clueless boyfriend of hers that she isn't worth seventeen million pounds."

"And I can still tell people I wrote the book?" Charlie's voice sounded almost...sad. "No one will know about this ghostwriter?"

"They have to sign an NDA to work with me," Hugh said. "Most of them I found on previous retreats. They think if they write enough for me, I'll give them their own publishing deal. But the last thing I want is for the world of crime fiction to turn into another offshoot of the romance genre, so that will never happen. But they don't need to know that. It keeps them amenable. Ah, I see the breakfast being laid out, and I have to take a call in a few minutes. Shall we go inside?"

"Do you think maybe there's another editor at Red Herring who might be a better fit for me? Surely, someone who is just as good as you who might want to work with me on my book. I don't think the whole thing should just be scrapped, especially not the bit where the hero interrogates the murderer for sixteen hours. That's quite good *and* it's factually accurate."

"Oh, yes, all forty-eight pages of it – riveting stuff." Hugh's voice dripped with sarcasm. "And I don't negotiate or hand off my authors to other editors. I run the show, got it? Sign the contract or no one at Red Herring or any other publishing house will speak to you again. It's your decision. Right now I need to get inside."

The two men moved off, and the restaurant door opened and closed behind them. I waited for a few minutes, cuddling up to Oscar as the wind and rain picked up, and then when I was sure I'd given them time to head upstairs, I ducked out and raced around to the restaurant door.

So Hugh Briston was awarding Charlie Doyle a publishing contract, but only so he could use Charlie's status as an ex-detective to sell more books? And Hugh took advantage of young women as his ghostwriters while promoting his buddies to superstar authors? And all of this had been decided before we even set foot at Meddleworth?

If the world found out about this, Hugh Briston would be eviscerated. And I couldn't say I was sad about it.

CHAPTER TEN

Bree: I know it's early, but I just wanted to check, does Grimalkin usually eat her breakfast?

I put down a bowl of that meat you told me she likes, but now she won't come out from underneath Heathcliff's chair by the fire. She hasn't eaten anything since I got here, is that normal?

Like I said, she does look like she's full of rabbit or something.

Oh, and your mom came over with a stack of something called "wellness dust." She wants to put a display on the counter. I told her I had to ask you, and she went off in a huff.

$\mathcal{L}$uckily, when I entered the restaurant, I found it empty. Hugh must be on his call and Charlie might be in the bathroom or up in his room. A delicious smell wafted from the breakfast buffet, and the staff bustled around, setting out a spread that was worthy of a magazine shoot.

"Good morning, Mina," Donna greeted me as I passed through the door. "Were you and Oscar out for a walk?"

"Hello, Donna." In the bright lighting of the restaurant, I could see that Donna was impeccably dressed in a linen suit. She was watching the servers arranging sprays of flowers on the buffet. "Yeah, we stepped out for a bit, but we didn't get far when the rain started up."

"Yeah, the weather's supposed to be awful today, and a bad storm this evening. If trees come down the road may close, but at least it's cozy here at the castle." Donna swooped in on the buffet as soon as the servers moved away, and snapped a bunch of pictures.

"For the 'gram," she explained to me as she tapped on the phone. "If we want to appeal to a new, wealthier, clientele, we have to be *aspirational*. My parents never bothered with social media, but I've grown Meddleworth's following up to over twenty thousand."

"That's pretty impressive," I said. "I do the social media for my bookshop back home, although Allan helps me now that my eyesight has worsened. I've learned a lot from brands and my favorite fashion labels about creating an *experience*. A feeling. I do a lot of moody stacks of books and cozy reading corners and quotes about reading. Now, some people actually come to Argleton specifically because they follow our Instagram."

"That's exactly what I'm trying to achieve," Donna beamed. She handed me her phone so I could scroll through the Meddleworth feed. I couldn't make out a lot of the pictures but I was pleased to see that she was using alt tags with descriptions, so I could 'read' what the pictures were about. "It's working, too. Meddleworth is becoming a must-visit destination for luxury travelers. I did a lot of this back in London, helping luxury brands build a media presence. I never thought I'd get to use my skills on this place…"

She trailed off, her gaze focusing across the room, where Morrie had told me a portrait of her parents hung on the wall.

"I'm so sorry to hear about your parents," I said. "It must be hard to run this place without them. I know how much they loved it. I'm sure they'd be proud of what you achieved."

"I hope so." Her voice sounded far away. "It's not easy. They put so much of themselves into Meddleworth, but they just couldn't move with the times, and it just wasn't enough to balance the books. Sometimes I think that it was really the stress of this place that killed them. When I finally got a look at the books, the bank was ready to sell the place. I know some people in the literary community don't like the changes I've made, but all my parents writing and publishing friends came for was for the free booze and the scandalous parties. Meddleworth may have been the backdrop for every sordid literary scandal over the last two decades, but it never made my parents a cent. I've kept Hugh's retreats because at least they actually bring in money, but Meddleworth's days of offering cheap rates and free piss to anyone who claims to be a writer are behind us. I don't want to say that we're out of the woods yet, but things have been turning around."

"If the food is anything to go by, I think you'll be a millionaire." I grinned as I squeezed my sodden hoodie. "I have to go. I need to change before any of the other writers see me like this. I guess I'll see you for tonight's dinner?"

"Oh, no, actually, I'll be in today's sessions with you," Donna said. "I've been writing a book about Meddleworth House. It's not a mystery novel, more of a history of the estate and a memoir about growing up here, and all the famous literary figures my parents entertained. It's a little bit salacious, so I'm changing some names to protect the guilty. I was telling Hugh about it yesterday and he said that I could sit in on the classes and he'd take a look at the manuscript, see if it was something he might be interested in publishing."

"Oh, that's exciting." I couldn't help but think that Hugh Briston was probably the star of many of those salacious stories, but I didn't dare believe that Donna would portray him as the disgusting man he truly was.

"It *is* exciting. Oh, speaking of which, this is for you." She shuffled through sheafs of paper in her oversize leather tote and pulled out a memory stick. "Hugh said I had to give all the writers an excerpt to critique. I printed off copies for the others, but I remembered you said you prefer electronic."

"I do. Thank you." I'd specifically mentioned on my application that I preferred written material in a digital format so I could read them on my Braille note. But often people forget, and I was thrilled that Donna remembered.

"You're welcome. I hope you enjoy it. It was a lot of fun to write and research. And it will be great for business – people will flock to Meddleworth to stay in the place where all these real-life dramas took place." Donna lowered her voice to a whisper. "All we need is a famous murder here in the hotel, and we'll be set for life."

That's a weird thing to say.

"Er, yes, that would definitely help." I plastered a smile on my face. Having being involved in several murder investigations now, I wouldn't wish that on anyone. "Especially if the victim's ghost haunted the place."

"Exactly. You're a businesswoman like me. You get it. Sex and murder sell. Oh, and speaking of sex, I'm keen to hear more about your story, too. I read the first few chapters, and it's positively *racy*. I haven't read the other pieces. Hugh gave me copies, but I was up late last night chatting with him and Charlie Doyle in the bar so I didn't get time…oh, I must fly." Donna bent down and air-kissed both my cheeks. "I need to make sure everything on the estate is settled before I take the day off for the retreat. The storm warnings are getting worse, and I need to check that Jonathan has taken care of everything."

"See you later." I directed Oscar toward the staircase. The wind whistled down the chimneys and hammered at the castle walls. Jonathan hurried from the music room, Fergus trotting at his heels. I called out to him, but Jonathan was struggling into an oilskin raincoat and didn't reply. The front door slammed behind him.

He must have a lot to do with this wild weather moving in.

Oscar and I ascended the staircase. The guest wing burst with noise and movement as writers and other guests emerged for breakfast. Morrie met me on the staircase, sweeping me into his arms and planting a knee-weakening kiss on my lips.

"I woke up and you weren't there," he whispered. "Heathcliff and I had to make our own fun."

"I'm sure you managed," I said with a smile.

"Oh, I managed so well that Sir Stroppywimple needs to lie in for a bit." Morrie bit my earlobe. "But we missed you."

"Quoth and I went to visit the ravens. They're in an aviary, and he wants me to help him set them free."

"Oh, our poor bleeding-heart birdie." Morrie sighed, wrapping his arms around my waist, holding my body against his, my back perfectly notching against his chest. He rested his chin on the top of my head, and I smelled Heathcliff's peaty scent clinging to him, mingling with his zesty grapefruit and vanilla in a way that drove me wild. "What are you going to do about it?"

My fingers trailed down his arm, stopping at the heavy gold watch on his wrist. Morrie had expensive designer taste, and I liked that he took the time to look good. "I'll have a word to Jonathan about them. That's all I can do." I dropped my voice as Charlie slipped down the stairs beside us. I couldn't see him glaring at us, but his animosity rolled over me like a wave, making me shudder. "I overheard an interesting conversation between Charlie and Hugh Briston."

"I'm all aflutter in anticipation."

I turned around to kiss his cheek. "I'll tell you about it later. I want to get changed quickly. I'm soaked through."

"You are rather wet, but I thought you were just pleased to see me."

I gave him a playful shove as I darted away from him. "I'll meet you downstairs. Save me a seat, okay? And Quoth, too."

Morrie blew me a kiss. "You'd better hurry, gorgeous. I've heard you don't want to miss the chef's pancakes."

"Noted."

I directed Oscar to our suite, which was right at the end of the hallway. I dug the room key from my pocket and opened the door. Heathcliff's snores rattled through the room. He'd be grumpy that he missed out on pancakes, but I wasn't going to risk his wrath by waking him up.

The grim light streaming through the windows illuminated a huge canvas on the wall – a bright-colored wave that made me think of what a song might look like if it were painted. I stood admiring it for a few moments, drinking in the colors and features I could still see, and I remembered Quoth telling me that Kelly-Ann, the art tutor he was taking classes with, painted all the work in the rooms.

That's so cool. I think Quoth will enjoy learning from her.

I dug through my suitcase and pulled out the outfit I'd especially chosen for today – a pair of black slacks, a white silk vintage slip I'd altered into a top, and a black pinstripe blazer that might've once been part of a public boy's school uniform, which I'd adorned with pins. The fashion designer in me knew that it was important to make a good impression for Hugh Briston, and I wanted something that said I was a serious writer but also let my personality shine.

It turned out that Hugh Briston was a mean, sexist pig, and now I didn't give a fuck what he thought of me. But that wasn't going to stop me from looking cute and feeling confident. *If that sexist pig can teach me something about preparing my manuscript for publication, then this retreat will be worth the trip.*

I ran a brush through my unruly hair and swiped on some lip gloss.

As I headed for the door, I noticed a light flashing in the closet. I lifted one of Morrie's suits aside and found the room safe. I run my fingers over the face to feel the Braille labels on the buttons. The one beneath the flashing light read "A" for "Armed."

It was then I remembered that Morrie was wearing a watch around his wrist in the hallway, and he hadn't said anything about Quoth stealing a watch from the safe. Surely he would have noticed when he looked in there this morning?

Weird.

It's probably nothing. I bet that Morrie let Quoth take that watch. He's always had a soft spot for Quoth. He may act like he doesn't care about anyone, but James Moriarty would give all his gold jewelry if it made one of us smile.

I shrugged my shoulders, kissed a snoozing Heathcliff on the forehead, and hurried downstairs.

As Oscar and I moved down the hallway, I couldn't help but be distracted by the sound of voices in an adjoining room. After overhearing the conversation between Hugh and Charlie, my ears pricked for more juicy gossip.

I made Oscar stop, and strained to hear. But I couldn't make out words – echoing along the hallways was the loud, unmistakable sound of a woman's moans!

CHAPTER ELEVEN

*T*he woman moaned again, and I recognized the voice of Christina, the nice, if slightly desperate, gothic fiction writer I met last night.

"Harder," she cried. "Harder!"

Her words dissolved into incoherent groans, drowned out by the rhythmic creaking of a piece of antique furniture being tested beyond its capabilities.

Wow, now I see why she's with that Killian guy. I stood in the hallway for a moment, impressed by their stamina. *By the sounds of those noises, he knows his way around a woman's body. And she's so into it. Good for her—*

But I was shocked from my thoughts a moment later when a male voice called out her name.

And it was *not* Killian's voice.

It was Hugh Briston.

This must be the 'call' he had to take, I thought. *Hugh Briston is sleeping with one of the writers, and someone who he has promised a job.* That was a pretty big misuse of his power.

Before I knew it, my feet were carrying me and Oscar down the hall to the door where the noises were coming from. I pressed my ear against the thick wood of a suite door and listened.

"Yes, Christina!" Hugh cried. "Milk my cock with that tight pussy of yours."

Eewwwwwww. I do not want to hear this.

"Oh, Hugh, Hugh….um, is your testicle supposed to look like that?"

"It's fine. It was a printing press accident from many years ago. Don't worry about it. Now, do that thing with your hips…that's it…"

Why am I listening again? Oh, that's right, I can't bear to ignore a mystery, and Hugh Briston's affairs are definitely a mystery.

The creaking and moaning grew louder, more frenzied. They both let out a strangled cry, and then the creaking stopped. Christina sighed happily.

"Hugh, that was amazing. I can't believe this is happening. I've dreamed about this day since I got my creative writing degree. I know that you and I will be great together, in publishing and in life. I'll tell Killian that I no longer need him. Maybe I'll be able to get out of paying him the royalties—"

"Don't worry your pretty head about any of that," Hugh cut her off abruptly. "This contract is just between you and me. All you need to do is sign here…and here…"

There was a shuffling of papers, and then Christina said, "All done!"

"Wonderful. And don't forget what we discussed. No telling anyone about our contract until the retreat is over. You're now a Red Herring author, but that doesn't automatically guarantee success – you're going to have to work for it."

"I will earn it. Hugh. I'm ready to work. I'll work harder than I ever have—"

"I believe you. Off with you now. I have to get dressed. There's a dining room filled with tedious writers I have to meet."

Christina made a noise of disappointment. There was the

sound of shuffling. *They're probably putting on their clothing and heading down to breakfast...*

Shit. I'm right in the middle of the hallway. They'll notice me—

As if on cue, light footsteps began to walk across the room, heading toward the very door where I was hiding!

I didn't even think. I whirled around, grabbed the nearest door, and pulled. It was a guest room and was locked. But right next to it was a narrow door with no carved decoration or number. It must be a supply closet.

I yanked it open and threw myself and Oscar inside, closing the door silently behind us just as the door to Hugh's room creaked open. Oscar pawed at my feet. I held his collar and scratched his ears to keep him quiet while I listened. Christina walked past and headed back to her room, and a moment later, her shower started running. My heart pounded against my ribs.

Hugh's door slammed so hard that it made the wall shudder. The stairs creaked as he headed down to the restaurant. Christine was still in the shower. I counted to sixty with my heart in my throat before pushing the door open and letting a rather rattled Oscar lead us downstairs.

Quoth and Morrie were waiting at a table when we walked into the restaurant. Quoth got up and went through the buffet with me to tell me what each plate of food was and help me get the servings onto my plate. (Buffets can be a bit of a nightmare when you're blind.) The staff gave Oscar a water bowl and some mashed vegetables, and I removed his working coat so he could sit happily under our table and enjoy his feast.

"You're blushing, Mina Wilde." Morrie's breath grazed my ear as I tucked into my towering plate of pancakes, caramelized banana, berry coulis, and tiny breakfast sausages. "Is this about that salacious conversation you overheard, or did you and the Ornery Bear upstairs get up to a little mischief?"

I glanced over my shoulder, but I couldn't see the faces of the people at the tables nearest to us. "Are any of the other writers nearby? Or Donna?"

"No."

"Okay, well, you're not going to believe this…"

Morrie and Quoth leaned toward me. I told them everything I'd overheard Hugh and Charlie saying, and the exchange between Hugh and Christina upstairs.

"I'm glad Heathcliff isn't here, because he'd acquaint Hugh's facial features with a critical item used in the building of walls," Quoth said.

"Who am I hitting with a brick?"

"It emerges from the deep," Morrie intoned as Heathcliff collapsed into the seat next to him. His dark hair hung in his eyes, rumpled from sleep. He looked amazing, as always.

I was in the middle of whispering the story to him again when Donna clapped her hands for attention and invited us writers to begin our day of workshops with Hugh in the library, and the artists to start their classes in the east wing.

Quoth picked up his sketchbook and kissed my cheek as he headed off toward the art gallery and studios. Morrie closed his spa brochure with a happy sigh and said, "Take a good look at me now, gorgeous. By the time you see me at dinner, I'll be an entirely new man."

"Do I get a choice of which man you'll be?" I asked. "Because I pick Jason Momoa."

"Very funny." Morrie took my hand and kissed my knuckles, sending a delicious, flirty shiver down my spine. "I have a full day of treatments – hot stone massage, cupping, LED facial, salt scrub, seaweed wrap… I shall emerge from my cocoon a radiant butterfly, whereupon you will delight me with your salacious tales. And maybe we'll create a little salacious tale of our own."

"And I'll be reading in the snug right next to the library," Heathcliff said, holding my hand in his and curling his fingers through mine protectively. "If that oaf so much as claims you have a comma out of place—"

"I'll be fine." I kissed his rough, stubbled cheek. "I can handle myself."

I picked up my Braille note, and Oscar and I followed the other writers into the beautiful castle library. I'd seen it on the brief tour Jonathan had given us yesterday, but now I paused to take in its magical atmosphere.

The wind howled against the windows outside, but one of the staff had lit a blazing fire in the ancient inglenook fireplace. Bookshelves made of dark stained wood lined the walls, crammed with books and objects d'art. Mismatched armchairs were arranged in a semi-circle around the fireplace, with tables stacked with pens and stapled manuscripts, and the staff were putting the finishing touches on a buffet of brownies, cakes, and biscuits along one wall.

Even if Hugh was a dick, this weekend was definitely going to be memorable. Meddleworth House really was an experience!

We crowded around the fire and chose our places. I sat on one end of a studded leather Chesterfield. Oscar stretched out at my feet, enjoying the warmth of the fire, even though he remained alert in case I needed him. Christina sat beside me, her arms loaded down with notebooks. Killian took up a chair at a table behind her, part of the group but not. I didn't like him there, watching us. He wasn't a writer, so I didn't understand why he was here. But I wouldn't make a big deal out of it when Christina was the only person who'd been nice to me.

Charlie Doyle sat at a seat on the end, and I couldn't help but notice he was wearing an ugly mustard-colored tie. Vivianne draped herself across a chaise lounge under the windows. With the grey light from the windows and the orange flickering of the fire, I could see that she was wearing a strangely low-cut, figure-hugging dress, which seemed an odd choice for the cold weather and the nature of our retreat, but I remembered she was here to enact her revenge plan, whatever that was. All night last night she sat across from Hugh at the table, loudly correcting him every time he talked and, according to Morrie, making his face 'as red as your beautiful derriere after a session with my belt.'

Donna perched on a high-backed chair, her long legs folded, looking far too elegant to be a writer.

Only when we were all seated did Hugh Briston storm into the room. He lowered himself into a wingback chair beside the fire, facing us. He was a silhouette against the dancing flames, but I could *sense* his scowl from here. I don't know why he did these retreats if he hated them so much.

The sound of Christina's cries of ecstasy and Hugh's grunts flashed in my memory.

Oh, that's right. I do know why he does these retreats. They're his recruiting ground for young, female writers.

"I hope you are all prepared to work," Hugh barked without so much as a greeting. "During this series of workshops, I will impart every piece of wisdom on the crime fiction genre I have gathered during my long and prestigious career. We will discuss every subgenre of crime fiction, from procedurals and amateur sleuths, to the traditional British and the gothic, right through to the psychological thrillers so popular on the bestseller charts in the post-*Gone Girl* era. We will dig into prose, themes, suspects, red herrings, and the construction of a compelling mystery. You will work harder than you have ever worked in your life. In the afternoons, you will have a few hours to write, and in the evenings, we will gather in this room after dinner to read and critique each other's prose from the day."

Great. I can't imagine anything more fun than having Hugh eviscerate my rough draft in front of everyone, except perhaps opening the time travel room in Nevermore Bookshop to find oneself in the Cretaceous era in the middle of a T-rex mating ritual—

"As you know," Hugh continued, "at the conclusion of the

retreat, I will select one author with promise and offer them a publishing contract with Red Herring Press, under my tutelage. This spot isn't simply about getting out one book. It's about building a career for the right author. This is no lovey-dovey safe space – you are competing against each other for your future. I suggest you bring your best work."

Except that you already gave the contract to Charlie Doyle, and you're going to make Christina write it, so what's the point in stringing everyone along?

Beside me, Christina shifted excitedly in her seat. She was so certain Hugh was going to make her the next big thing.

Should I tell her what I heard? I don't want to shatter her dreams, especially not on the first day of the retreat. But surely the sisterhood means that I need to tell her that Hugh is taking advantage of her?

I decided to talk it over with the guys at lunchtime. Right now, I was here to extract whatever useful information I could from this workshop. I leaned forward, my fingers poised on my Braille note, as Hugh waved something around. It was small and thin, but I couldn't tell what it was, and I wasn't going to ask him.

"This is my lucky pen," he said as he raised the object in the air. *Okay, so it's a pen.* I couldn't see it, but it glinted where the firelight caught it, and I had a feeling it was some expensive gilded thing. "It's made by one of the finest fountain pen makers in the world. We writers have our superstitions, our rituals. Every bestselling manuscript I've edited, every Bram Stoker or Edgar Award winner, has been *caressed* by this pen..."

The way he said the word caressed made me throw up a little in my mouth.

"I'll be using this pen liberally over the course of the week to show you the errors of your prose. Now, let's discuss how superstitions play into mystery and crime novels. If we look to the queen of crime, Agatha Christie..."

For the next hour, I was transfixed as Hugh talked. He may have been an utter dickweasel, but he knew so much about the crime genre and books in general. My fingers flew as I typed on my Braille note, barely pausing as he moved breathlessly from one topic to the next.

"...of course, the supernatural in a mystery shouldn't become a distraction, but must instead become another suspect to be examined with logic and reason by the detective. Supernatural forces must have a clearly defined motive and means for committing the murder. It cannot take over the story, lest we devolve into the realm of fantasy. And that leads me into our discussion of your works."

He leaned over and picked up a stack of papers from beside his chair, and began to toss manuscripts at the writers in the room.

"I have marked up the first two chapters of each manuscript, so you can see what I'm talking about when I refer to the use of atmosphere in invoking the—"

A manuscript hit me in the chest.

"Excuse me, Mr. Briston," I cut in, hating how cajoling my voice sounded. I desperately wished I didn't have to say anything, but knew that I'd miss out on half the useful information from the retreat if I didn't get this straightened out. "As you can see, I'm blind. I'm going to struggle to read handwritten notes you've made on my text. When I signed up I asked for notes to be electronic so I can read them on my Braille note and I was assured—"

"I'll make things simple for you, Ms. Wilde," he said in a haughty voice. "The only note I have made on your story is to put a huge red cross right the way through it."

You fucker.

His words hit me like another gut punch. I gasped as the air drove out of me. I actually couldn't breathe. Never in my life had I heard such a deliberately cruel comment directed at me.

Dimly, in the background, I'm aware of a loud thump and a string of curse words, but I was too busy trying to force air back into my lungs to pay much attention.

I trembled with rage and humiliation. My cheeks flared with heat. Oscar, sensing my distress, growled at Hugh, but if the publisher noticed, he was too busy being a smug bastard to say anything.

It was bad enough that Hugh said all those awful things to me last night, but did he have to humiliate me in front of all the other writers?

"I'm sorry, Mina," Christina whispered as she patted my leg. "Hugh is the best in the business. I enjoyed your story, but if he says it's not any good, then it's probably better that you find out now rather than make a fool of yourself trying to get it published."

"Especially since you can't get your facts right," added Charlie Doyle snootily. "Because the police would never allow someone to escape from jail and then forgive her because she found the real murderer. In my thirty-three years on the force, I never heard of that, and as for your medical examiner character—"

"No one will want this dribble," Hugh scoffed as he japped his fingers at my manuscript pages. "Mommy porn and talking ravens don't belong in serious crime fiction—"

"How dare you?" a deep, rasping voice boomed across the room, dripping with malice.

A voice that never failed to make my knees weak and my panties wet.

Heathcliff.

He stormed into the room, exuding Big Heathcliff Energy. Beside me, Christina let out an excited yelp. Killian leaped from his chair and ran to intercept him, but Heathcliff tossed him aside like an Instagram influencer after a cryptocurrency scandal. My beautiful, furious, monster of a boyfriend came to stand in front of Hugh Briston's chair.

"Who the devil are you?" Hugh said with a sneer in his voice, but I detected a hint of terror.

"I'm the man who's going to invert your ribcage and tie your arteries into fleshy balloon animals. I'll teach you for talking down to Mina like that."

"Heathcliff, what are you doing?"

I remembered now that Heathcliff said he was in the reading snug opposite the library. The library door had been open, and he must have heard everything Hugh said to me. Heathcliff grabbed him by the collar, yanking Hugh off the chair.

"Put me down!" Hugh bellowed.

I tried to grab Heathcliff's leg, but Oscar – sensing a tense situation – placed himself between me and the two warring men. I couldn't get around without crawling over Christina. Panic rose inside me.

With his free hand, Heathcliff tore the front page off my manuscript and screwed it up into a ball.

"Open wide," he growled at Hugh. "You want to treat my girlfriend that way, I will literally make you eat her words."

"This is unheard of!" Hugh spluttered. "What this the meaning of this mmmmmoooo mmmmphffffffffffff…"

"That's it." Heathcliff stuffed the ball of paper into Hugh's mouth. He held Hugh's jaw shut while the man wriggled and writhed in a vain attempt at freedom. "You'd better start chewing, because you have many more pages to go. Oh, but first, I think we need to sweeten that mouth of yours."

He grabbed a handful of potpourri from a bowl on the mantlepiece and shoved the leaves into Hugh's mouth alongside the now mushy paper.

"Mmmmmmmmmmmphffffff!"

Hugh's cheeks puffed out and his eyes were so wide they reflected the firelight.

"Jonathan!" Donna yelled. "Come quickly! There's an incident!"

"What are you doing?" Christina cried. "You're hurting Hugh."

"That man should be arrested." Charlie Doyle rose to his feet.

"I'll hold him until the police get here. I know how to deal with criminal scumbags like this—"

"No one's calling the police," Jonathan growled as he stepped around Oscar and inserted himself between Heathcliff and Hugh. Jonathan grabbed Heathcliff's wrist and somehow managed to loosen his fingers from Hugh's throat. "Come on, big guy. Out of here with ye."

Heathcliff dropped Hugh, who collapsed into his chair, coughing and spluttering as he spat out gobs of paper and dried leaves.

"He was trying to kill me!" Hugh rasped out, clutching his throat.

"Damn right, and I'll do it, too!" Heathcliff growled as Jonathan dragged him away. "You can't treat Mina this way. I will *gut* you, you fiend. I will unbraid your DNA from the inside!"

"I'm sorry, everyone. I'll just…" I got to my feet. My trembling legs barely kept me upright as I fumbled for my things and Oscar's harness. "I'll get out of here. I'm so sorry for disturbing…"

I ran out of the room just as Christina burst into tears.

I found Jonathan dragging Heathcliff down the hallway. "I've half a mind to listen to that imperious sod and call the coppers," he was saying to Heathcliff. "But they won't come out here in this weather. The bridge down the road floods and cuts us off. Besides, I understand your anger. That Hugh Briston is a right royal sod. The way he talks to people, especially women, I'd like to box him around the ears my own self. I can't believe Donna invited him back here, after the way he treats Meddleworth. But then, she's only interested in his money."

"Jonathan, I'll take Heathcliff to our room," I said. "I'm sure you have jobs to be getting on with and don't need us in the way."

"Aye, I do." Jonathan tipped his deerstalker to me. "I'm heading out to check the water supply. Would ye like me to walk Oscar?"

"I'd love that." I removed Oscar's working jacket and harness and handed his lead to Jonathan. "Thank you. Bring him back to my room when you're done. Oh, and I was wondering about the ravens in the aviary. I um…volunteer for a raven sanctuary at home and I can't help but think the cage is too small for those birds. Surely they should be able to roam free?"

"Aye, I agree." Jonathan bowed his head. "But try telling that to Donna. All she sees are smelly old birds who shit on the outdoor furniture and steal guest jewelry. But they're too intelligent to be stuck in that cage for long. Why, I bought a fancy new lock for the cage but even so, that little blighter got free last night and came right inside. He flew away before I could lock him away again. So don't ye worry, miss. They'll all be free before you know it."

I wish with all of my heart that was so.

As soon as Jonathan was out of earshot, I grabbed Heathcliff by the arm and started dragging him toward the stairs. Tears streamed down my cheeks. I was so angry and upset that I walked into the corner of the doorway.

"Why did you do that?" I hissed at him.

"You heard what he said to you," Heathcliff's hand brushed my cheek. He yanked me to a stop and rubbed at the tears on my cheek. "That horrible man did this to you. He's a fiend and a liar. You are a brilliant writer, Mina Wilde. And I would never lie to you. I will always tell you the truth, which is that you're amazing, and I can't bear seeing you cry. I hear him hurting you like that and every bone in my body wakes up and goes into attack mode."

"This isn't 1802! You can't just kill a man for dishonoring your woman. I'm probably kicked out of the retreat now. And maybe it doesn't matter if I'm a good writer or not if I wrote a book that no one wants to read. Hugh seems to think—"

"I don't give a toss what Hugh thinks. Why do you want to waste your time sitting in a room for a week with a man like that?"

"Because being a writer is more important to me than Hugh Briston's hurtful words," I yelled.

Heathcliff staggered backward, as if I'd slapped him. "Mina…"

My name sounded ragged on his lips.

"I can't even talk to you right now." I whirled around and fumbled my way up the stairs to our room, far far away from Heathcliff Earnshaw's well-meaning wrath.

CHAPTER TWELVE

J was lying on the bed, replaying the horrifying end to the morning's workshop and my harsh outburst at Heathcliff, when the door to our suite banged open.

"I came as fast as I could." Morrie sank down on the bed beside me. He was naked from the waist up, and a bunch of spiky crystals were stuck to his chest. His face was covered in something sticky that smelled like lemon cake. "What's the matter, gorgeous?"

"How did you know I was—" But then I saw the dark shape crowding the doorway.

"I texted him," Heathcliff growled. "Even I will use a mobile phone in an emergency."

"I was in the middle of my transformative crystal treatment, which honestly was a bit of a rip-off." Morrie picked crystals off his pecs and dropped them onto the bedside table. "Why would I need to transform when I'm perfect the way I am?"

I laughed at his ridiculousness, but it made the lump in my throat grow two sizes. I looked away, dangerously close to bursting into tears.

Morrie wrapped his toned arms around me and pulled me in

close. I rested my head against his chest, breathing in the scented oils rubbed into his skin. "Tell me what happened, and I will decide on Heathcliff's punishment."

"It's not his fault," I said. "Well, I mean, it's partly his fault. He attacked Hugh Briston in front of everyone. But he was just standing up for me. Hugh…well, he didn't listen to the accessibility accommodation request I made and he said…"

I trailed off. I didn't want to talk about what Hugh said.

Tap-tap-tap. Rain pattered against the windows. The storm was brewing.

"You wouldn't believe what that rotten man said to her," Heathcliff growled. He picked knickknacks off the fireplace one by one and hurled them into the grate. "We know Mina is a good writer. And he had the *nerve* to say horrible things about her in front of everyone."

"As Mina pointed out, that *is* the purpose of a critique group," Morrie said. "Are you sure you aren't overreacting…"

"He called her book 'mommy porn' and said that Quoth didn't belong in the story."

"Did he now?" Morrie bolted upright and rubbed his hands together with glee. "Why didn't you say so? We'd better get busy. I saw a rather impressive armory next to the meditation room, but it might take us some time to find a sword long enough to go all the way up his sphincter—"

Tappa-tap-tap-TAP-TAP.

"Croak!"

That's not rain on the window.

"Quoth's outside!" I cried.

"I should bloody well hope so. I texted him, too." Heathcliff stomped over to the window and threw it open. A gust of wind whipped inside, followed by a huge black bird that toppled onto the flagstones. It stood up and shook the rain off its feathers, glaring at Heathcliff and hopping about madly. He tried to croak, but he had something long and thin in his mouth. Morrie bent down and took the object and pocketed it so Quoth could hop over and yell at Heathcliff.

I can't believe you left me out there! After everything I went through to get it. The weather's awful and I've left all my clothes in a tiny bathroom in the art gallery in the middle of the most delicate part of the process to—

"Calm down, Birdie. Mina needs you."

Black feathers flew in all directions. A moment later, Quoth sat on the other side of the bed, rubbing my back as Morrie held me. "Mina, what happened?"

"I'll tell you what happened," Heathcliff raged, kicking at the pile of clothing and shoes Morrie had tossed in the corner of the room. "Hugh Briston happened. I'm going to *get* him. I'm going to use the Geneva Convention as a to-do list. I'll wait until Jonathan's back is turned and then I'll fill every cavity in Briston's body with assorted cheeses and use his pelvic bones as crackers for a delicious ploughman's platter—"

"—with his toes as olives?" Quoth piped up.

"Yes. And his pancreas creamed into a nice pâté..."

"No, no, silly boys," Morrie purred. "You don't bring down a man like Hugh Briston with cannibalism. You ruin him with *brains*. With what Mina overheard this morning, we already have everything we need to ruin him—"

"That's good." Heathcliff started tossing Morrie's crystals into the fireplace. "We'll tell the media that he's taking advantage of young, impressionable female writers and arranging his contracts in advance of the retreat. The publishing world will relish the scandal and—"

"Stop!"

The three of them froze, mid-maniacal scheme. Quoth winced.

"As much as I appreciate the sentiment behind this, I have a few problems. First of all, we don't know if he was taking advantage of Christina," I said, ticking off my fingers. "She strikes me as someone who knows *exactly* what she's doing with Hugh. And if Killian isn't aware of their affair, then that's none of our business.

"Second, no one is killing anyone, and you can't go around saying things like that. Charlie might be a tool, but he's right – what you did *is* assault and if the police could get here through the storm, they'd likely be involved by now. Hugh is an important man, and if I want to be a writer, he's going to be part of that world whether I like it or not. He doesn't like my books, fine. He's allowed not to. Not everyone likes the same thing."

"But he upset you."

"He did. It hurts when someone rubbishes something you've worked so hard on." I shrugged my shoulders. "Especially when so much of the story is about my own life and my struggles and my love for the three of you. But it is an unusual book, and if I want to be a published author then I have to be okay with critics and reviewers saying mean things about it. Sometimes I might even agree with them."

"But what did you mean when you said being a writer is more important than how Hugh treats you?" Heathcliff demanded.

I hid my face as the lump in my throat returned. "I didn't mean it. I was upset."

But I could barely get the words out without a wobble in my voice.

Quoth sat down beside me and gathered me into his arms. "I get it."

Heathcliff and Morrie fell silent. A moment later, Morrie said, "We should leave Mina and the birdie alone."

They turned and left, shutting the door softly behind them. Quoth nuzzled into me. His skin smelled of fire and soot. There must be a fireplace in the art studio.

"Don't you have to get back to your class?" I asked.

"It can wait. You were saying about becoming a writer being important to you, and why you're so determined to sit through Hugh's abuse?"

"All I ever wanted to be was a fashion designer," I sniffed. "That's who I thought I was. And if I really still wanted to do that, then I would pursue it, even as a blind person. But I've reached peace with my decision to leave that part of my life behind me, except for occasional forays into Shakespearean costume design for village events."

Quoth nodded, his obsidian hair falling over my shoulder as he held me tighter.

"When I started to write the book, it all came flooding back, you know? The sheer *joy* of creating, of taking my ideas and making something that other people could enjoy. I think...I think this is what I'm meant to do with my life. Books have always been important to me. They were a place I could escape to when the world got tough, and I think I'm meant to write stories like that for other people. I want to create worlds for people like me, for people who were feeling a little lost, to be a place to escape for a while and come back feeling confident and empowered and like magic could be real."

"Magic is real, especially the magic you wield, Mina." Quoth kissed my fingers. "And I'm not just talking about the waters of Meles. I think you've found the thing you're meant to do with your life. Your story is beautiful, and when people read it they will find hope in dark places, the same way you gave me hope in my darkness."

"Aw, Quoth." I squeezed him back. "I can't take credit for any of that. *You* are the one who saved *me*."

"Remember when I hid all my artwork up in my room? Heathcliff and Morrie said it was too morbid and that no one else would ever like it. I thought that was true. I didn't think I had a place in the world. But then you dragged my painting downstairs and put it on display, and Jo bought it. A *real person* bought it. I don't think I'd ever been so happy as in that moment."

Tears flooded my eyes again, but this time they were tears of joy. Quoth's artwork was deeply personal – a way for him to escape into himself and avoid the outside world – a world where he didn't always fit. I pushed him to share his art with the world because I knew that you don't have to be a shapeshifting raven from a gothic poem to feel like you don't belong.

To know that I did the right thing…

That meant everything.

"That's how I felt when I got my acceptance letter for the Meddleworth retreat," I sniffed. "That maybe I had found my place in the world. But it turns out that it was a lie. I'm here because I tick a box for the organizers, not because I'm good."

"You *are* good, and I'm not just saying that because I love you. I say that because you make me feel less alone. If you can make anyone who reads your work feel like that, then that's what matters. Not what idiots like Hugh Briston say. If you want this badly enough, Mina, you'll find a way. You always do."

Quoth cupped my cheeks and brought my face to his, claiming my lips. Quoth's kiss was tender, searching, making sure that this was what I needed.

And it definitely, definitely was.

We rolled over on the bed. I pulled him on top of me. He leaned on his elbows as he kissed me, his fingers softly stroking my hair and my cheek.

When I could see well enough to distinguish emotions from people's eyes, I always remembered how Quoth looked at me like he couldn't quite believe I was real, like he was the luckiest man on earth every time I was near him. I couldn't help being addicted to the thrill of being worshipped. What girl wouldn't be?

Nowadays I couldn't make out the details of his fire-ringed dark eyes beyond a very blurry pinprick of light when the lighting was just right. But I didn't need to see his eyes to know what he was thinking. I felt his worship in the way he moved with me, the brush of his fingers, the way his mouth wandered over my body, dancing warmth into all the dark and hidden places inside me, the shadows between bones.

I held up my arms, and Quoth slid off my vintage slip. He moaned as his hand cupped my breast, and he bent his head. His hair fanned out across my skin, and my lungs caught when his tongue brushed the curve of my breast. His eyes lifted to mine as he took my nipple in his mouth, and those little flames inside his irises burned with all the reverence he saved up for me.

I bet the other writers aren't enjoying their afternoons this much.
Well, maybe Christina...

I arched my back, rising up to meet him, to beg him for more. He murmured my name as he crawled down the bed, his long artist's fingers tugging my slacks down over my knees. Our mouths collided again as his fingers slid up the inside of my thigh. I moved my legs wider as he hooked a finger into my cotton panties and slid them down my legs, too.

He sat up and wrangled my panties over my feet, tossing them into the mess of clothing in the corner. His mouth twisted into his beautiful smile as he looked down at me. "You're so beautiful," he whispered. "Inside and out."

The lump in my throat grew and bubbled with heat. I wanted to say something, but Quoth tightened his grip on my hips and bent down between my legs. My breath stuttered as the heat of his tongue melted against me.

He groaned as he devoured me, like a man lost in the desert who'd stumbled into a Wetherspoons. I rolled my hips into the pressure of his tongue, and Quoth groaned. His fingers danced across my stomach and splayed out, holding me down as he did amazing things with his tongue that undid all the knots I'd tied up inside me.

My hands tangled in his hair, feeling the way the satiny strands fell through my fingers like water, too beautiful to be real. A line from Poe ran through my head as Quoth's tongue worked its dark magic.

Yet if hope has flown away
In a night, or in a day,
In a vision, or in none,
Is it therefore the less gone?
All that we see or seem
Is but a dream within a dream...

Quoth was my dream within a dream – a being of such fragile magic that the simple act of touching him might make him turn to dust in my arms. His hair rippled across my stomach, and I swear that his tongue was made of fairy dust, the way it made me...

He worshipped me with slow, purposeful strokes. The pressure built inside me until I was a shuddering mess beneath him. My hands twisted in his hair. I ached. He cupped me beneath my arse, angling me upward to devour me, deeper, hungrier. He wrote his magical spell into my skin and I...I could do nothing but cry out and tumble headlong into the enchantment.

I became a being of pure ecstasy in that moment, and as the magic crested and ebbed away, I held Quoth, pressing his cheek to my chest, relishing the hardness of his muscles, the silk of his hair, the very *realness* of Quoth.

"I'm sorry that you're missing your class," I murmured, gripping him under the arms as he crawled up my body so our mouths could meet again.

"That's okay. The afternoon was free time to work on our projects, and the studio is open late, so I'll go back this evening. This is much more important. And fun."

The ache inside me that he had sated grew anew, becoming a swirling tempest that demanded an offering. I opened my legs, and Quoth notched his narrow hips between them. I traced my fingers over the beautiful tattoos cascading down his arms. They were no longer images to me but just splashes of color that delighted my eyes.

I raked my hands over his body, taking in every hard line and firm curve of him, wishing I could commit touch to memory in the same way I could with sight. I wanted to drink in this moment whenever I felt that I didn't belong.

He slid into me with slow care, our bodies perfectly melding together. As he pushed a little deeper, ribbons of color danced and shimmered in front of my eyes, turning everything around us to darkness – part of my eye condition that used to be scary but was now just a beautiful part of me.

The world softened and darkened around us, cocooning us in this moment.

"You feel like silk," Quoth whispered, his mouth trailing kisses over my neck as he pushed deeper. My body shimmered like fireworks beneath his touch, his...*everything*.

Quoth sat back on his knees, dragging me closer, making sure he still remained impaled inside me. He gripped my ankle and moved my leg onto his shoulder. Then he did the same for my other leg. I gasped as he leaned forward and thrust further into me.

He'd changed the angle. He thrust deeper, and with my legs over his shoulders, his pubic bone rubbed against my clit. My fingers tore at the sheets as the pleasure built inside me with every thrust.

I don't remember ever trying this position before, but damn, it was my new favorite.

I braced myself against the bed, my legs tightening against his shoulders with every thrust to work myself against him. I wanted him deeper still, so deep that we could no longer tell where one of us ended and the other began.

And as he brought me to the very center of that tempest once more, I held on tight and knew, in my heart of hearts, that no matter what happened with my writing, I would always be a goddess to this man, and that was enough for me.

CHAPTER THIRTEEN

*Q*uoth stayed with me in the suite for the afternoon. We ordered room service, and I read Donna's manuscript (It was an interesting history of the castle, but it had quite a few odd spelling mistakes, like the word 'prick' when she meant 'pink', which caused me no end of giggles. Something about the errors felt familiar to me, but I couldn't quite figure out what it was). I wrote her some notes.

After that, I got to work on the writing assignment Hugh had set for us – to write the first chapter of a mystery plot where someone's paranoia is justified. Quoth took a hushed call from Morrie in the bathroom, which I could only assume was him assuring the other two that he'd fucked a smile back onto my face.

He flopped across the bed, doodling in his sketchbook while I read out sections as I wrote them, and he helped me polish the piece until I thought it was something worthy to share.

At 6PM, Heathcliff and Morrie returned with a well-exercised Oscar and a tray of food from the kitchen. "We thought you wouldn't want to eat in the restaurant with the others," Heathcliff said. "We thought maybe we would go to bed early while Quoth went to the painting studio and you could choose a terrible movie and—what are you doing?"

I pulled out a woolen, figure-hugging dress in a deep red color that I loved. "What do you think? I'm getting dressed for the evening critique session."

"But I thought you weren't going to see that man again."

"No, *you* said I'm not seeing that man again." I held my chin high, tucking my hands behind my back so none of them could see them trembling. Oscar climbed up on the bed and nuzzled me. "I paid for this course. I'm going to get everything out of it that I can, even if Hugh is a terrible person. Speaking of Hugh, he hasn't got Charlie to lock you in a supply closet as a citizen's arrest?"

"Donna gave Heathcliff a stern talking to, and he's not allowed in the same room as Hugh Briston for the remainder of our stay, but it's all smoothed over," Morrie said as he picked at the roast lamb. "Donna was rather strict. I bet she'd wield a whip with precision and cruelty."

"I don't think you should go to this thing tonight," Heathcliff nodded at the window, where the wind and rain rattled the panes. "Not during a dangerous storm."

"It's not storming *inside* the house."

"You never know. Zeus could strike a lightning bolt through the window that fries Hugh and blasts your eyebrows off."

"Good." I wiggled my eyebrows at him. "Then I wouldn't have to get them waxed."

Heathcliff flopped into the armchair by the fire. "There's no reasoning with you. Fine. You go to your flagellation. I'm going to sit here and mope until you get back."

Quoth slid out of bed and went over to the food they'd laid out. "This looks incredible. I'll have to eat quickly. I want to get back to the studio."

Morrie brushed past him to swoop in on the last stuffed

Yorkshire pudding. "You have fun, birdie. I'm returning to the spa for my LED facial."

"See? We've all got exciting evenings planned." I grinned as I speared a Brussels sprout and popped it into my mouth. "Oh, by the way, what was that object you gave to Morrie?"

"What object?" Quoth flicked a strand of obsidian hair over his shoulder.

"When you came in the window earlier, you had something in your mouth. I think it was a metal object?"

"Oh, that. The birds gave me back the strap to Morrie's watch. Apparently, it wasn't shiny enough to interest them." Quoth nuzzled my cheek. "Stop worrying about my nonsense and eat up. You don't want to be late."

~

"*A*re you sure you don't want me to go with you?" Quoth asked forty minutes later as we walked down the stairs. "Having your work critiqued can be pretty harrowing. I've had to sit through some awful group sessions at art school."

"It's fine." I flashed him a smile. "If I'm going to be a published writer, I need to get used to reviews and critiques. And I'm happy with what I wrote today."

My stomach squirmed. I was lying to myself. I didn't particularly want to go back into that room with today's writing and listen to everyone bash it. But being critiqued was how artists learned to be better. I'd given a few people my manuscript to read – Heathcliff, Quoth, and Morrie, of course. Mrs. Ellis. Jo. Grimalkin. They all loved it, except for Grimalkin, who declared that the mother of the most famous poet to have ever lived wouldn't stoop to reading anything unless it was written in Homeric Greek, and then she threw up a hairball on top of it.

But that wasn't the same as getting feedback from actual writers. And I was not going to let Hugh and Charlie get to me. I'd decided that once I finished the course, I would make a complaint to Red Herring Press. Hugh may be good at spotting a thriller, but he definitely shouldn't be able to behave the way he does. It was the right thing to do.

"We believe in you." Quoth kissed my head. "If you need me, I'll be in the art suite. Just send me a text and I'll come running."

"And I'm locking Heathcliff in the meditation room," Morrie said, dragging Heathcliff in the direction of the spa. "He won't be anywhere near the library this evening."

"Good. Thank you."

I hugged the copies of my new chapter close to my chest and directed Oscar to head in the opposite direction, toward the library. Halfway there, I stopped beside one of the arched gothic windows to peer out across the estate just as lightning forked across the sky, illuminating the bedraggled gardens. Rain pelted down and the sculpted trees bent so far over in the wind that they looked like they would snap in half.

Another flash of lightning, and I caught sight of an enormous black bird soaring past the window. With the other ravens locked up in the aviary, it had to be Quoth. And he was carrying an object in his beak. I wondered if he was bringing more of Morrie's prized watch collection to his feathery friends.

Be safe out there, birdie.

It really was an awful storm. Even though I didn't like Hugh or any of the other writers, I did love being inside the ancient castle during this horrible weather. I felt safe and protected by the old stone walls and the cozy fires everywhere.

The door to the library was closed when I arrived. I tried the handle, but it was locked. I knocked against it. "Hello, are we still doing the—"

The door flung open, and Donna stood on the threshold. "Oh, Mina, good. We didn't know if you were coming. I'm locking us in while we do our critique, just to avoid any…disturbances."

"That's completely fair. I'm so sorry for Heathcliff's behavior. It was completely uncalled for."

"Please, I'd like to have a swarthy, magnificent hero like that to defend my honor! Besides, it's far from the craziest thing that's ever happened here at Meddleworth," Donna said with a smile in her voice. "Just ask Jonathan – he'll tell you some stories. His knowledge of this place has been absolutely invaluable for my book. Although you and your fellows may merit a mention. I went to find Heathcliff earlier and talk to him about his behavior, only to have one of my staff members tell me that she found all three of them huddled under a pile of towels in the laundry cupboard, holding a secret meeting."

"They were?" That was odd. I thought Heathcliff said that he texted Morrie and Quoth, but Donna is saying that she saw them together?

"Yes. They looked quite guilty when I shooed them out. And Heathcliff took his tongue lashing well." Donna stepped aside. "Anyway, let's put it behind us and enjoy our evening."

Unsettled by the strange story she'd told me, Oscar and I followed Donna inside. The library lights were dimmed, with only a couple of lamps near the fire casting low shadows. But the fireplace burned with a bright orange fire, flames leaping and dancing, casting eldritch shadows across the walls. I was drawn to the fire immediately. My eyes loved dancing light and my body craved the crushing warmth of a fireplace in the middle of a storm.

I sat down in my same seat from earlier, beside Christina on the couch. I twisted myself and could just make out the edges of people where the light touched them. Everyone was in the same places as earlier.

No one spoke.

There was a booming knock at the door. Diana got up and let someone in. Hugh strode across the room just as thunder rumbled through the old castle walls. "Donna, I think you'd better call the police. We have a thief in our midst."

Donna leaped to her feet, her voice concerned. "What are you talking about, Hugh? Has something been stolen?"

"It certainly has." Hugh slammed his fist down on the tiny table next to his chair. "I had my lucky pen with me during this morning's lecture, and after that brute attacked me, it disappeared. Someone in this room stole it."

"Now, now, I'm sure it just rolled away in the tussle." Donna snapped her fingers. "I'll call Jonathan to look for it after we've finished our critique session. In the meantime, I'll get you another pen. We have hundreds in the staff supply cupboard."

Donna left to get him a pen, and Hugh slumped down in his chair. "I can't believe I'm expected to work in these conditions…" he muttered. "First, I'm attacked by a crazed psychopath, and now I'm stuck in this creaky old castle during a storm with a rotten thief who stole…hey, what's this doing here?"

He held up an object. It glinted in the firelight.

"Why Hugh, I believe that's your pen." Vivianne smiled smugly. "Isn't that exactly where you left it earlier? Perhaps you're going senile in your old age."

"I'm not senile. This pen was *not* here earlier. Nor was it under the chairs or stashed behind the fire poker. I checked the room *thoroughly*. Someone swiped it and then put it back as some kind of childish prank. I tell you that this won't do." Hugh turned to Donna, who'd just returned and was locking the door again behind her. "If this sort of nonsense continues, I will move the retreat to another location next year."

"Please don't do that, Hugh," Donna's voice rose an octave. "This place wouldn't be the same without your legacy."

"If you want to continue to make money off my legacy, then you need to treat me with respect and punish whoever it was who stole my pen. I hope you all have brought pages for us to edit," Hugh said. "Otherwise, I will be happy to return to the bar."

Judging by the slight slur in his voice, he'd spent too much time in the bar already.

"I'll go first." Vivianne swooped to her feet. She was wearing another flowing gown, and she moved around Hugh as if she was going to stand in front of the fire. But at the last moment, she flopped down into his lap.

"Get off me, woman!" Hugh tried to shove her off, but Vivianne held firm.

"Now, now, Hughey baby, you used to love it when I did this." She held up her pages. "Shall I delight them all with a tale of true love…and revenge?"

Vivianne began to read. She spun a tale about a wife of a philandering husband with a misshapen testicle. The wife was plotting revenge. It was strange because the story was a completely different style from the ho-hum female detective story she submitted. It was brilliant, in fact.

As she read, Hugh Briston squirmed in his seat. Even I could see he was uncomfortable and disturbed by what Vivianne was reading.

"Don't you like it, dear?" Vivianne cleared her throat pointedly. "This is the first chapter of my brand new novel. It's a real page-turner. Shall I keep reading?"

"You can't…"

"Yes please," I couldn't help but pipe up.

Vivianne kept reading as she detailed a revenge plot that involved murdering each of her husband's mistresses. The story was told in alternating timelines – one as the wife was plotting, and the other as the police were putting clues together to send the husband away for the crimes.

I had the distinct feeling that it was at least partly autobiographical.

This must be part of her revenge? And Hugh certainly didn't seem to appreciate it.

After Vivianne stopped reading, Charlie and Christina offered a few critiques. Hugh remained surprisingly mute.

"I'll go next." Christina moved to stand in front of the fire-place beside Hugh. She glanced over at him and then, in a clear, musical voice, she started to read her piece.

It was stunning. It truly was. In a few words, Christina managed to weave a haunted atmosphere of a crumbling manor house and a mother and her young child struggling to find their place in the world as a sinister shadow lurked just out of reach. It might have been the impact of the storm raging outside and the roaring fire, but I felt transported into her story.

When she finished, I clapped.

"That was beautiful," I said. "You do a lot with so few words. It's a real gift. I think you could probably expand on the boy's point of view, and maybe find a way to make his voice sound younger. After all, he doesn't have the history with the manor that his mother does. To him it might be exciting to have all that space…all the games he can create…"

"I suppose it was *fine*," Charlie grumbled. I remembered that he was listening to the work of the woman who would be rewriting his police procedural for the market. That had to sting.

"It's better than fine." Vivianne sensed a weakness and swooped in for the kill. "That's award-winning writing right there. Too bad she's going to be wasted at Hughey Boy's publishing house, where he'll have her ghostwriting books for useless male writers like you and sucking his cock under his desk. Isn't that right, Hugh?"

"Vivianne, shut your face," Hugh snapped, but his words didn't have the usual venom behind them. Whatever secret message Vivianne had delivered in her work, it had got to him.

"That's not true at all." Christina glanced around the room. "You might as well tell them, Hugh. There's no sense keeping it until the end."

"Tell us what?" Donna asked.

"Hugh's promised me the contract with his publishing house,"

Christina beamed. "He told me this morning that he's going to publish my book. Didn't you, Hugh?"

"He did?" Killian glanced at Christina in surprise. "Why wasn't I there? I'm supposed to be present for contract negotiations."

"It's not true," Charlie said, his words barely audible over the wind howling outside. "He's giving the contract to *me*. You might be helping with a little spelling and grammar, but my name will be on the front cover."

"Oh, she'll do more than that," Vivianne smirked. "Hugh will have her rewrite the whole thing. We've all read your manuscript, Charlie. It's so full of boring details about how the real police work and cliche 'good cops' lusting after innocent female victims that it'll put the public to sleep. By the time Hugh's done with it, not a single word will be yours."

"But I don't want that!" Charlie yelled. "I want you to publish my own book, the one I've been working my arse over for the last ten years. Hugh, if you don't let me write my own book, we've got a serious problem."

"My only problem," Hugh shot back, "is why you're making a fuss when I'm offering you a big wad of money and a chance at stardom. You were *supposed* to keep these deals quiet, so the other participants wouldn't complain that I was playing favorites."

"You *are* playing favorites," Vivianne pointed out. "The only reason you haven't offered pretty little Mina the same deal as Christina is that you're terrified of her brawny boyfriend. And what about Donna? Surely you've noticed that she's attractive? She has tits and an arse, after all, which is all a woman needs to tempt you—"

"That's enough now," Donna scolded. "If you must know, Hugh has told me that he wants to publish my history of Meddleworth as part of a new non-fiction line."

It was then that I noticed how close she'd moved her chair to Hugh. She was practically sitting in his lap.

"But what about me?" Christina's voice wobbled. "What about all the promises you made to me? You said I was going to be the next literary star!"

"Oh, for pity's sake," Vivianne scoffed. "You haven't changed at all, have you, Hughey? Do you want to enlighten the girl, or should I?"

"Vivianne, don't start—"

"Dear, sweet, *naive* Christina, the contract you signed on your knees isn't for the six-figure publishing deal you dreamed about. It's to be a servant for hire as one of Red Herring's ghostwriters. You'll write books for men like Charlie over here, who, let me guess, has already signed a contract."

"How do you know?" Charlie demanded.

"But...but..." Christina spluttered, jerking to her feet. "But Hugh, *I* signed a contract for my book. You said that if I went to bed with you, you'd get me to the top of a bestseller list."

"I did promise that," Hugh said. "But I never said it would be your name on the cover."

"What did you just say?" Killian stormed around the table. "You coerced an innocent young woman into bed with you to make a contract behind my back? *I'm* her agent. I need to vet every contract. You're playing with fire, Briston."

"She didn't take much coercion," Hugh bit back with a brittle laugh. "Your little girlfriend might appear timid, but she's been bouncing on my cock since the moment I arrived at the estate."

"I'm going to kill you!" Killian roared.

"Not if I get there first!" Charlie jerked from his seat.

A great gust of wind slammed against the house, rattling the windows and shaking the lightbulbs in their ancient sconces.

"I really do think that everyone should calm down..." Donna said. "We can take a break, maybe have some food, and return when we're a little—"

She broke off with a scream as all the lights went out.

CHAPTER FOURTEEN

Someone cried out in shock. Another person yelled angrily.

For me, the effect wasn't as dramatic as it was for the others. Some of the contrast in the room disappeared, but the bright flames had already dominated my vision, and now they stood even brighter. Every part of the room not in the fire was a dark, fathomless shadow.

I gripped Oscar's harness tighter as fear ballooned in my chest. I was still on edge from the argument and threats that had erupted before we were plunged into darkness.

It's just a power cut. It's nothing to be worried about.

Shadows moved in front of the fire – silhouettes against the leaping orange wall. It seemed that everyone was moving about. Oscar and I were the only ones not on our feet.

Oh, and Hugh. I could clearly make out his silhouette still sitting in his chair. And someone bending over him, but I couldn't see who.

"What's going on?" cried Vivianne.

"Someone's playing a rotten trick on us," Charlie snarled. "I'll find the little punk and—"

"It's not a trick," Donna said calmly. I couldn't tell where any of them were standing. The room was so large and cavernous, and the wind outside so frightful, that I couldn't match voices to shadows.

"It must be the storm," Killian said. I thought it was him moving across in front of me, probably to reach Christina, but I couldn't be sure. Even with the fire roaring, I could still only make out vague silhouettes. "Jonathan said that the storm could get bad enough that we might lose power for a bit. I bet that old man is out there right now, putting on a backup generator and rousing the kitchen staff to make us some hot cocoa."

"You're not wrong. Jonathan really is the backbone of this place. Unfortunately, the generator was on the fritz," Donna moaned. "Jonathan was trying to fix it but I don't know how it went. It might be a while before the lights come back on."

"What do we do now?" Christina sniffed.

"Killian has a point about the hot chocolate. We need to stay comfortable and warm. I'll get the fires lit in all the rooms and hand out candles. We can cook chocolate and soup over the open flames without power. And I'll instruct the kitchen staff to put on some cold supper in the dining room," Donna said. I could hear her voice growing fainter as she moved toward the door. "We have candles and oil lamps we can hand out, and hot water bottles if the heating doesn't work."

"That sounds amazing." I stood up, directing Oscar in front of me. "We'll go wait in the dining room for the other guests. If any of you would like to hold my hand, Oscar will take us to the door so we don't bang into anything in the dark."

"Excellent idea, Mina."

Christina's tiny hand slotted in mine, and, after a bit of shuffling and moaning, everyone else held hands in a chain behind us. Oscar let out a little yip of excitement. He enjoyed having so many people relying on him. He trotted off in the direction of the doorway, steering us around the tables,

Chesterfield sofas, and the towering antique globe that dotted the floor.

I reached the door and pulled on the ornate handle. It didn't work. I tried pushing instead.

"The door won't move," I said.

"Oh, of course. I locked it earlier so our meeting would remain private." Donna's clothing rustled as she fumbled in her pockets. "I have the key here somewhere. Ah, here it is. We had these new electronic locks installed, and you just have to point the key at the lock and it will...hmm, it's not working."

"The storm must have damaged the security system," I said.

"Well, that's not my problem." I recognized Charlie's disgruntled voice. "How are we going to get out of here?"

"I don't know," Donna said. "I thought they had a battery backup. There's a manual switch but it's on the other side."

"This is ridiculous. I can't believe I'm locked in a room in a sodding storm with this bunch of cretins," Charlie snapped.

"There isn't even a liquor cabinet in here," whined Killian.

"Let's use one of those big statues as a battering ram and break the door down ourselves," Charlie suggested. "I did it all the time when I was a detective—"

"No!" Donna snapped. "Those statues are priceless, and the door is solid oak. No one is getting through that—"

Thunder cracked outside, so close that the whole building rattled. I bit down my fear.

Something thumped against the door. Christina shrieked.

"What was that?"

"Someone tripping over something?"

I placed my ear against the thick wood and listened. Another dull thud. Someone was knocking on the door.

"...okay in there?" I faintly heard a voice. I was pretty sure it was Jonathan, but it was barely audible against the din of the storm and the sniping writers.

"Jonathan, it's Mina," I yelled, hammering my own fist against the door. "We're all fine, but there's no power and we can't open the door."

"Mina?" Jonathan's voice came back. "…be okay…get my tools…stand away from door…"

The knocking stopped. I gripped Oscar's harness, and he took me deeper into the room. Thunder clapped again, and forked lightning lit up the windows. I wanted desperately to crawl under a table, pull my hoodie over my eyes, and hug Oscar close.

I wish the guys were here with me.

I thought of Quoth flying around in this weather earlier. *I hope they're okay.*

A moment later, Jonathan shouted something through the door again, followed by the sounds of banging as he worked with his tools to get the lock open. Meanwhile, the writers took the opportunity to take up their bickering again.

"You shall be hearing from my lawyers!" Vivianne shouted at Donna. "This house is a death trap. As soon as we get out of here I'm leaving, and I'll never come back! I've got what I came for, anyway. My revenge is complete. But you, young lady, you will be beggared by the time I'm done with you!"

"Please, Vivianne," Donna said, her voice calm despite Vivianne's hysterics. "I can't control the weather. I only just got this place solvent again after my parents died. If you consent to sit down and give me a no-holds-barred interview for my book, tell me more of Hugh's juicy little secrets, I'd be more than happy to make it worth your while."

"I can't believe you slept with Hugh!" Killian yelled at Christina.

"You said that I should do anything to get ahead," Christina yelled back. "So I did. I got the deal, didn't I? I signed the contract this morning—"

"But you didn't read it before you signed it, did you?" Killian sneered. "I thought writers were supposed to be voracious readers. But you were too busy gobbling Hugh's speckly old man dick to worry about a trivial little thing like reading your contact. Who knows what you've signed on for."

"I never would have gone behind your back if you hadn't been so overbearing," Christina sobbed. "Well, Hugh betrayed me, too. Now I'm going to be writing Charlie Doyle's police prostitute book instead of seeing my own work in print—"

"It's a police *procedural*," Charlie pointed out huffily. "The only prostitutes in my work have hearts of gold, but they couldn't qualify for a badge. They haven't done the requisite training courses. And I think you'll find the finer details of evidence collection extremely invigorating—"

"Argh!" Christina shrieked. "I can't believe this! I don't want to read a word of his shitty book. Killian, get me out of this."

"As far as I'm concerned, you've made your own mess," Killian shot back. "But Hugh Briston promised me I'd get to make this deal. It would have been my ticket to bigger clients. But he cut me out, and I'll make him pay."

"Where is Hugh?" Charlie demanded. "I thought he followed us over here?"

"He's sitting by the fire. I can see his silhouette." Killian stalked off in that direction. "Oi, Hugh. I have a bone to pick with you about the boning you gave my girl. I thought we had a deal—"

The door hinges creaked. With a final bang, the door flung open, and Jonathan burst into the room, holding aloft a bright torch.

"Is everyone all right in here? The generator's poked, so I'm afraid I cannae get the power back running, but we do have lots of candles and a few flashlights—"

"No," Killian cut in. "We're far from all right."

"Yes, we are most displeased with the service." Vivianne sniffed. "I demand a car be sent for *immediately* to take me far away from here."

"And I want a drink!" Charlie demanded.

"All right, all right, keep yer hair on." Jonathan swirled the flashlight around all of us, lowering the light when it rested on my face. "You're all going to come with me to the dining room. All the guests are congregating there. Where's Hugh?"

"He was right here with us, wasn't he?" Donna peered around. "Hugh?"

"I see him. He's still here by the fire." Killian called from the other side of the room.

Jonathan came over to me. "Do you need any help to the dining hall, miss?"

"Not at all." I patted Oscar. "He knows the way. I'll follow you and the others, and if we can be of any help whatsoever, just let me or my boyfriends know—"

"Um, Hugh won't be coming with us," Killian said in a strange, croaky voice.

"Oh, stop being so ridiculous, Hugh," Vivianne scoffed. "This is no time to act as if you can't bear to be in the same room as me—"

"That's not what I mean." Killian's voice rose in pitch. "Hugh physically cannot follow us out of this room unless someone shoves a stick up his ass and waves him around like a lollipop. He's dead."

"Don't be absurd," Vivianne said. "He's probably found a secret stash of whisky and has been polishing it off while the rest of us have been dealing with the actual problem."

I wanted to point out that Vivianne was the one wailing about suing while Donna and Jonathan had actually been dealing with the storm, but I bit my tongue.

Because I had to have misheard Killian, right?

"I'm sorry, Killian," I called out. "But did you say that Hugh was hurt?"

"No, I'm saying he's *dead*. He's...he's sitting right here in the chair beside the fire. And he's not moving."

CHAPTER FIFTEEN

I directed Oscar to follow Jonathan across the room to the roaring fire. Hugh's chair was still visible, and his body slumped into it, just the way he'd been when the lights first went out.

He can't be dead.

That's impossible.

Christina's keening wail pierced my ears.

"Huuuuuuugh, noooooooo!"

Okay, I guess he's dead.

I moved in front of Hugh's body. I couldn't see any more than his outline with the bright fire all around, but the fact that he wasn't moving or sneering at me made it pretty clear that he'd expired. There was a stillness to the scene that was profoundly eerie and all too familiar.

I had encountered enough dead bodies that I could taste the presence of death in the air.

I swallowed. *This can't be happening.*

This was supposed to be my holiday from Nevermore Book-shop and Argleton and all the strange and kooky goings-on there.

I wasn't supposed to encounter a dead body. Especially not of the publisher who I'd wanted to impress.

"He's dead, he's dead!" Christina wailed, running around like a chicken without its head.

"There's no reason for us to panic," I said, reaching out a hand to her. "It's very sad, but Hugh must've had a heart attack or another medical emergency. We might not have heard him cry out over the storm—"

"This is no heart attack," Charlie Doyle's voice wavered as he bent to inspect the body. "And that's why you need a copper with years of experience to write good crime fiction. I could tell from just a glimpse that we're looking at a murder."

"We can *all* tell that, Charlie," Killian huffed. "Hugh's been stabbed in the throat with his own fountain pen."

CHAPTER SIXTEEN

"*H*e's been murdered," I whispered, half to Jonathan, half to myself.

Another murder.

"Noooooooo!" Christina cried. "Huuuuugh, why must someone so talented be taken from us so soon?"

"Come off it," Killian snapped. "No one's buying your fake empathy."

I bent down to stare across Hugh's throat into the fire. I hadn't noticed it before, but from this position, the silhouette of the long pen was visible. I was thankful that I didn't have to look closely at the blood. I wished my friend Jo was here. She'd immediately see all kinds of clues that I couldn't understand.

"Murdered?" Jonathan's voice turned incredulous. "This is no time for stories. I've got my work cut out for me getting the generators working and checking on all the guests. I don't have time for no jokes—"

"It's no story, Jonathan." I took his arm and turned him in the direction of the fireplace. "That pen didn't get there by accident."

Jonathan lifted his flashlight. His breath came out in a low wheeze. "You're right, lassie. No one could have done that accidentally."

"We have to call the police." My mind whirred through the events of the evening. "We need to get out of here and secure the scene. We have to tell them that someone in this room is a murderer."

"But that's absurd!" Vivianne gasped.

"Well, he didn't stab himself in the throat," Charlie said, grabbing the flashlight from Jonathan. I watched his silhouette bend over Hugh again, inspecting the body before moving outward to the rest of the scene. "Even if he'd wanted to do something so stupid, the angle is all wrong. And this blood splatter here—"

"Blood splatter analysis is notoriously unreliable." I couldn't help myself. I didn't like Charlie taking over from me. He wasn't a detective anymore, and he had a business relationship with Hugh, which meant that he wasn't exactly impartial. "You need to step back. We can't risk contaminating the evidence, especially given the circumstances. We all need to exit this room and wait for the police to get here."

"I just tried them," Donna said. The light from her phone screen danced in the gloom. "But I can't get a call to connect. My phone has no reception."

I heard a beeping noise behind me. Killian said in a strangled voice, "Mine's out, too."

"I'll try the house landline—"

"No good, Donna, I'm afraid. It's down, too. Ain't no one's getting through in this weather," Jonathan said. "In fact, no one's going anywhere, either. We're completely cut off. The coppers will have to wait until the rains recede."

"But...but...I can't be trapped here with a murderer." Vivianne made a rush for the doors, but Jonathan stepped in front of her.

"I'm afraid that none of you will be allowed to move freely in the castle," he said. "You see, this room was locked from the inside by Donna's key. This is the only way into and out of the room. Which means that one of you is the murderer, and it's my job to make sure you don't hurt no one else."

CHAPTER SEVENTEEN

"*M*ina!"

I glanced up from my chair in the private dining room at the sound of the familiar voice. A willowy figure darted through the gloom. Two strong arms wrapped around me, and a vanilla and grapefruit scent tinged with expensive massage oils invaded my nostrils.

"Morrie." I buried my nose into his fluffy robe. *Is he wandering around the castle in the middle of a thunderstorm, with a murderer on the loose, wearing nothing but his spa robe? That's very on-brand.* "It was horrible."

"It's okay now, gorgeous. I've got you."

"Sir, if ye want to be with her, ye won't be allowed to leave this room," Jonathan said as he stood near the door. "Mina is a suspect."

"I understand." Morrie squeezed my hand. "If you need any help running security, let me know. This lot look like the kind of feral psychopaths who would gnaw their own arms off just to use their arm stump to club a fellow author to death."

"Excuse *me*, young man," Vivianne snapped. "I won't be

gnawing anything except Donna's head in court after I sue her for keeping me forcibly detained."

Morrie grinned innocently and held me tighter.

Beside me, Donna stoked the fire to life in the small, private dining room, which Jonathan had decided would serve as our makeshift jail cell. Christina, Killian, Charlie, and Vivianne all sat around the antique oak table, glaring at each other with unbridled suspicion. Firelight flickered over photographs on the walls – scenes from previous writers' retreats and raucous literary galas hosted by Donna's parents.

The hotel's other guests were being roused from their rooms to gather in the restaurant, where the staff was serving supper. A delicious scent of hot chocolate, steaming soup, and warm, sliced bread that was supposed to be for tomorrow's breakfast wafted through the air. My stomach rumbled, but I didn't know if we'd get to share in the joy.

After all, one person in this room was a murderer.

Murderers didn't deserve hot chocolate.

"I came running as soon as the lights went out," Morrie squeezed me tighter. "Are you okay?"

"I'm fine." I shuddered. "But it was awful. I was sitting right across from Hugh, and then we got up to try the door, and...he was attacked. It was pitch black. I didn't see anything."

I can't believe someone was murdered right under my nose and I didn't even hear it.

"But we all know that seeing isn't everything." Morrie's long fingers slipped effortlessly into mine. "You must have other impressions."

I thought back to the chaos of the blackout. Everyone was talking and moving around at once. The storm and the bickering were so loud that I couldn't recall any other noises that seemed out of place. I did remember someone brushing past me when we all got up to go to the doorway, heading in the opposite direction.

But it could have been any one of the writers trying to move around the space.

I shook my head. "No noises that I could associate with his actual murder. I was holding Christina's hand when we moved across the room, so I don't think it was her, but…when I think about it, the last time I heard him speak was right before the lights went out, so it could have been anyone, before we moved away to the door." I shook my head. "But we're not solving this murder, so it's a moot point."

"We're not?" Morrie leaned in, his voice hinting at mischief.

"We're *not*," I said firmly. "I'm a suspect. It wouldn't be right."

"Why, Mina Wilde, you shock me. As if you've ever cared about propriety." Morrie lowered his voice. "You certainly didn't care about propriety when I had my cock buried in your a—"

"I'm *serious*. We're going to sit here in this room and wait for the police to come."

"You can't stay out of this. I can see your mind working. You're already trying to figure out who had a motive to kill Hugh."

"I am not." My face flushed with heat. "I mean, obviously Christina, and Killian, and I guess Vivianne, too—"

"Mina? Mina's okay?" Quoth's worried voice reached us. I glanced toward the door just as he ran over and threw his arms around me.

"She shouldn't be allowed all those men in here. I don't want the one in the suit, or the oafish one, anywhere near me," Charlie cut in. "After all, they probably killed Hugh."

"As much as I'd like to claim credit for such a public service," Morrie said, "it's awfully difficult to kill someone from behind a locked door."

"But those *do* sound like the words of someone deflecting blame from themselves," I added.

"There's the Mina I love," Morrie grinned.

"Charlie did remind me that we're missing Heathcliff."

Morrie stood up and kissed the top of my head. "I'll find him."

Jonathan moved to block the door. "I said, you're not to leave this room."

"You have one guest not accounted for," Morrie said. "I'm going to find him. You're welcome to come with me if you wish, but that will leave the room of would-be murderers unguarded. Is that what you want?"

Jonathan thought for a moment, then tossed Morrie his lamp. "Report back here in fifteen minutes whether you find him or nay, or I will lock them all in this room and come after you."

He looked ferocious. This must be awful for him. Jonathan loved Meddleworth. This castle had been his home his entire life. I think it hurt him to know that someone was murdered here, as if something beautiful and sacred had been sullied.

Morrie took the lantern from Jonathan and disappeared down the hallway. Quoth snuggled up to me. He smelled of smoke.

"Is there a fire in the studio?" I asked. "That must be so cozy."

"The studio?"

"The art studio. You smell like you've been near a fire." I sniffed his hair.

"Oh. Er...yes. There's a little stove in the corner. It's toasty warm in there. I was so involved in my work that it took me a while to realize that the power had gone off."

Even in his human form, Quoth's raven eyes meant he could see much better in the dark. So he probably could have kept painting even without power.

"I've found him!" Morrie returned with a glowering Heathcliff behind him, wearing...

...a fluffy white robe?

I throw my arms around him. "I'm so glad you're okay."

"Okay? Why wouldn't I be okay? I'm better than okay – I've just had the toxins sucked from my body—"

"You...*what?*"

132

Nothing coming out of his mouth made any sense.

"I found him in the spa's contemplation room," Morrie said. "He was lying on a massage bed, covered in cucumber slices and scented oils, sound asleep."

"This is a lovely robe." I fingered the fluffy hem. "And…Heathcliff, are you wearing slippers?"

"They said I had to," he muttered as he plonked himself into the chair beside me.

"Who said?"

"The woman who rubbed me down with oils." Heathcliff leaned back and crossed his feet on the table, fluffy slippers and all. "Is there any whisky?"

"Who *are* you and what have you done with Heathcliff Earnshaw? I've never even seen you in a robe. And you slept through the storm of the century and a murder—"

Heathcliff bolted upright. "Murder? Are you okay? Is Quoth—"

"I'm fine," Quoth said.

"We're all fine. But Hugh Briston isn't fine. Someone stabbed him with his lucky pen."

"Can't say I'm all that cut up about it. That man wouldn't know a real writer if they stabbed him in the throat."

"You can't say that!" I hissed.

"Too soon?" Heathcliff's voice tinged with dark humor.

"Did you hear that?" Vivianne piped up. "Did you hear that man's callous disregard for my poor, deceased husband? Surely he must be on our suspect list."

"If you can propose a way he got into the room, then sure," I shot back. "But he wasn't even anywhere near the library at the time of the murder. I'm sure security footage will place him in the contemplation room until the moment that the power went off. As we've already established, the room was locked at the time, so only one of us inside the room could be the murderer."

"And what's this about your poor husband?" Donna piped up.

"Half an hour ago, you were celebrating getting revenge on him by publishing a book that obviously contained half-veiled personal details about him. You're hardly a picture of innocence."

"Vivianne is protesting a little too much," Charlie cut in. "I believe she's the murderer. In all my years as a detective, it was usually the spouse who did the deed."

"Hugh and I have been divorced for five years," Vivianne scoffed. "If you want to look for a suspect, I suggest you ask the person he was sleeping with, although that could be any young woman in this room."

"Not me." I was proud to say it.

Neither Christina nor Donna made such a claim.

"But Christina was just sleeping with Hugh to get a contract," Killian said. He sounded as though he was trying to convince himself. "It was business. She did it for me, for *us*, so I would get my deal. I don't exactly like how it happened, but neither of us would have any reason to kill Hugh because we got what we wanted—"

"That's not what Mina heard this morning," Morrie said.

I elbowed him in the ribs.

My face flushed even hotter as every eye in the room turned to me. "I took a walk outside before breakfast and I went up to my room just as everyone else was settling in the restaurant. I overheard Hugh and Christina...er...*in flagrante delicto*. And Christina said that she wanted to make sure that Killian didn't get a cut of her royalties with Red Herring."

"Christina, you didn't?" Killian spun around to face her.

"It didn't mean anything!" she spluttered. "He said that going to bed with him was the only way I could get to work with him."

"I don't care about the sex. I care that you tried to cut me off without a cent! After all the work I've put into you—"

"Work? What work? I'm the one who does all the work. I slave over the computer, night after night after long shifts at that gross Italian restaurant, surviving on stale popcorn and four hours of sleep, while you go to your industry parties and drink free booze and don't even lift a finger!" Christina was practically screaming now. "You don't deserve a penny!"

"They're both suspects. They both have a motive for killing Hugh." Charlie Doyle's chair creaked as he leaned back in it and crossed his own feet on the table, mirroring Heathcliff. "But I do not."

"That's not strictly true, though, is it?" I said. "I overheard you and Hugh talking outside this morning, too. With Hugh out of the way, you'd get another editor at Red Herring who would allow your book to be published – the book *you* wrote, not the ghostwritten manuscript that Hugh wanted."

"You think I would kill Hugh because he wouldn't publish my book as I wrote it?" Charlie sounded affronted. "It's ridiculous. If that's the kind of motive that you come up with in your amateur sleuth books, no wonder Hugh considered your work garbage. No, I'm sure that I'd have been able to convince him of the merits of my work. After all, he's a man of refined taste, and so am I."

I really, really don't like this guy.

"You said yourself that you worked on that book for years," I said, trying hard to keep my voice calm. "It had to hurt to have the publishing deal of the century, only to find out that it wouldn't be your book on the shelves."

"You're one to talk," Charlie shot back. "We all know whose book Hugh didn't think was even worthy of being critiqued, let alone published. All those things he said to you had to have stung. And aren't you bragging about how you're an amateur detective like the heroine in your story? Well, that would give you all the knowledge you need to pull off this crime—"

"Silence!" Jonathan yelled. "As far as I'm concerned, you're all guilty until the police get here to sort out this crime. No one in this room is going anywhere. I must protect this house and the people in it, and I will stand by this door all night and make sure that no one else gets hurt."

CHAPTER EIGHTEEN

"*I* need to go to the bathroom," Christina complained two hours later.

"I put a bucket for ye in the corner," Jonathan said.

Donna sighed. "Jonathan, please be reasonable. I'm not going in a bucket. The bathrooms are just down the hall."

"And what if you're the killer? What if I let you out to wipe your arse and you go into the restaurant and kill some perfectly innocent patrons?"

"This was a calculated, deliberate attack on Hugh," Charlie said in his I'm-a-police-detective-with-thirty-three-years-experience voice. "This killer has achieved their aims, and they wouldn't kill again unless it was to cover their tracks, so we can all bloody well go to the bathroom. I'm a detective, I know these things."

"Spoken like a true murderer," Killian shot at him. "Trying to make himself not a suspect."

"No, I'm just trying to empty my bladder without having to get my dick out for all and sundry to see."

"I don't see why I have to stay here," Vivianne said. "I'm tired and it's been a long night, and I'm not under suspicion. Surely I should be allowed to retire to my room?"

"Not under suspicion?" Killian scoffed. "The famously jilted ex-wife who swore revenge is not a suspect—"

"No one is going anywhere." Jonathan folded his arms over his chest as he blocked the doorway with his bulk. "We can't risk the murderer attempting to make a run for it before the coppers get here. So I suggest you *sit down*."

Jonathan said the last bit in a stern, terrifying voice. He meant business. And that meant that we were all trapped here.

Truthfully, I was going to need to go to the bathroom eventually, too. And no way was I going to use a bucket.

I know Jonathan was doing his job and protecting the castle, but we needed to get out of this room or Heathcliff was going to get stabby.

"Excuse me," I said. "My friends and I, we've helped the police solve several murders in my village of Argleton—"

"—liar—" Charlie coughed behind me. "The police don't work with amateur detectives."

"—and I've brought several criminals to justice. The cases were actually the inspiration for my book. Perhaps we could offer our services."

"For what?"

"To solve the crime." I rapped my nails against the table. "There were five people in the room at the time of the murder – Christina, Killian, Vivianne, Charlie, and Donna. Five suspects. It shouldn't be that hard to narrow it down to one murderer. If we know who did it, we could lock them up more securely until the police came, and the rest could go free."

"You forgot yourself," Charlie said sourly.

But I know I didn't do it. I gritted my teeth. "Fine. I'm a suspect, too. So that makes six of us."

"Perhaps we can all work together," Christina suggested, her voice brightening. "We're all mystery writers. We've all familiar with locked room mysteries, and at least *some* people in this room are innocent. Perhaps between us, we can figure out this crime."

"I'm intrigued by this idea," Morrie said.

"But how will we solve the crime?" Charlie asked. "We're trapped in the godforsaken room together with Attila the Hun at the door. We can't even inspect the crime scene, and as a retired detective, I know that the crime scene is the most important—"

"Morrie, Quoth, and Heathcliff can go," I said. "They weren't in the room with us, so they can't be suspects, and they've been involved in murder investigations, too, so they know what to look for—"

"Pffft, we're not fooled by that old trick. If we send your boyfriends, they'll locate the clues that incriminate you and destroy them."

"That only works if I'm the murderer," I said. "Which I'm not. But fine, then how about this? Heathcliff, Quoth, and Morrie go, and you go with them. They'll be Jonathan's eyes and ears and make sure you don't escape—"

"I'll be delighted." Heathcliff slammed his fist into his palm.

"And you can watch to make sure they don't tamper with any evidence. *And* you can lend your expertise as a detective with thirty years experience."

"Thirty-*three* years," Charlie corrected, but he sounded mollified by my suggestion.

Jonathan frowned. "I dinnae like this. You should all stay here for—"

"We could be here for *hours*," Donna said. "All night, even. None of us are going to go in a bucket."

"And if we decide to revolt, there's nine of us against you," Vivianne added, her voice thick with determination.

"If we get this figured out, then we can all relax, including you," Donna added. "You've been doing such a good job managing the estate during the storm, Jonathan. You deserve to be able to relax a little."

"And maybe have some whisky?" Heathcliff said hopefully.

Jonathan remained silent. "Fine," he growled. "The four of you can take a look at the murder scene. But don't disturb anything, and you're to walk straight to the library and straight back here again. You have twenty minutes."

Morrie stretched his quads on the table. "Excellent. I do enjoy vigorous exercise, as Heathcliff and Mina can attest—"

"We're leaving now." Heathcliff grabbed him by the scruff of the neck and dragged him to the door. Charlie followed, with Quoth at the rear.

Jonathan slammed the door behind them. "I hope I'm not making a big mistake."

Me too. I hope I didn't just send my boyfriends off with a murderer.

I glanced around the table at the shadowed faces of my fellow writers. Real life really was stranger than fiction when six crime writers would have to solve a murder to clear their name, with the murderer sitting at the table with us!

CHAPTER NINETEEN

"I've drawn this map of the room," Quoth said as he handed around sheets of paper upon their return exactly eighteen minutes later. "It's a little rough, as I wasn't allowed to go to the art suite for my supplies and I didn't exactly have a lot of time, but it will give you an idea."

I might've been imagining it, but Charlie seemed quieter than when they left the room, and I noticed he raced for a seat on the opposite side of the table, as far from Heathcliff as it was possible to get.

Quoth handed me a thick piece of card, and I was touched to find a tactile diagram of the room on it. Quoth had glued matchsticks and string and pieces of fabric to the paper to create a map of the room, the furniture layout, etc. I pulled out my Braille labeler and typed up labels for each of the writers and tacked them next to where each was sitting.

"We've done a thorough inspection of the room, and we can conclude that there were no other entrances or exits," Morrie said. "The main door was locked, as Mina, Donna, and Jonathan attest. There are two windows along this side of the room—"

"Directly behind where Charlie and Killian were sitting," Vivianne pointed out primly.

"Just because I sat near the window doesn't mean I'm a murderer," Killian shot back.

"No, but the fact that the murder victim was sleeping with your girlfriend rather suggests—"

"Oh, so you want to get into a discussion of who was sleeping with whose partner, because I've heard your husband's list of conquests is as long as your forked tongue—"

"I was pointing out the windows to show a possible entry point for an outside murderer," Morrie explained. "However, the catches are old and stuck and the windows could not be opened without the storm blowing through the room and alerting you all that they were open. Did anyone feel a breeze?"

No one said anything, but the writers must have been shaking their heads, because Morrie moved on.

"The only other point of entry is a small heating vent above the bookshelf, but this is not large enough for a human to pass through."

"So the murderer was definitely someone in the room," Christina's voice trembled.

"And we've established that Christina, Killian, and Charlie all have strong motives for wanting Hugh dead," said Donna. "But I don't."

"Hmmmm," I remembered something Donna had told me earlier. "You do, though."

"I do?"

"Yes. You inherited this estate from your parents, and the mountain of debt that came with it. You would have gone into more debt to build the spa and do all the expensive advertising. You're stretched thin financially, and you told me yourself that having a murder at Meddleworth would bring in more guests. Maybe you decided to engineer that murder yourself."

"That's absurd," Donna said. "I'm not so desperate for money that I would stoop so low."

"I wouldn't be so sure about that," Jonathan said from the doorway.

"Don't you mind Jonathan," Donna snapped, losing a little of her carefully crafted calm. "He's bitter because I've come into Meddleworth and started making changes. Well, if this place didn't change it would be bankrupt, and then where would we be? Hugh was giving me a boatload of money for my book on the mysteries of Meddleworth, on the condition it painted him and his literary events in a positive light. If I was going to kill someone, why him?"

"Because you specifically told me that the person who should be murdered would be 'high-profile'," I finished.

"I wasn't speaking literally!"

"Maybe not, but it's a motive enough for you to remain in this room." Morrie made some notes next to Donna's name on his map. "Now, who's next?"

"How about the woman who has said multiple times that her specific purpose in coming to the retreat is to get revenge on Hugh?" Charlie said in that self-satisfied voice of his, as if he'd already cracked the case.

"Please," Vivianne said. "You should stop contributing to this project. You're embarrassing yourself."

"Is that what Hugh did to you, Vivianne?" Morrie cut in. "He embarrassed you with his goings-on with young women and his frequent missteps when handling his affairs. You were young when he married you, weren't you? You were a writer. You gave him three novels you'd written to publish, and he made you sign over your rights to them to him. He made his fortune on your books, and you didn't see a single pound."

Oh, that's awful.

I couldn't imagine someone betraying me like that.

"And what of it?" Scorn dripped from Vivianne's voice. "So

my husband stole my work and make a fortune off it, and he didn't even have the decency to attempt to hide his multiple indiscretions. That's 'the business,' as dear departed Hughey Boy was so fond of saying."

"You made no secret of the fact that you hated him," I said. "I've read articles about you attacking him at a book launch. So why *did* you write a novel under a pen name just so he would accept you on the retreat? Why did you tell us all that you had a revenge plan? Could it be that you planned to kill him?"

"That kind of sentimental reasoning may work in one of your books, but this is the real world," Vivianne smirked. "My revenge was so much more enjoyable than simply killing the man. In fact, the person who killed him has robbed me of the joy of seeing my plan through to fruition, although they've possibly also helped me make millions."

Morrie leaned forward, steepling his fingers on the table. The Napoleon of Crime was intrigued. "I think you'd better explain."

Vivianne sighed, as though it was hell for her to be surrounded by such simpletons. "The book I submitted to be accepted was a ruse. I knew Hugh would recognize my writing and wouldn't accept my real work. Would you believe that I had AI software write it for me? It's amazing what computers will do these days. My real book is the one I read aloud tonight – it's an autobiography about my years with Hugh, all the rotten business deals he made, every desperate young writer he slept with and lured into his circle with promises of fame and fortune only to set them to work as writers for his real stars." Vivianne glanced over at Christina. "Sorry, my dear."

"I don't understand what you're talking about," Christina said through gritted teeth.

"Of course you don't. All those nights that Hugh came back to bed drunk as a skunk and told me about the mischief he got up to…I put it all in the book. And I even added some particularly personal details, like how one of his testicles is misshapen from when it got jammed in a printing press, and how he's got a birthmark on his ass that he likes people to lick. It gets him all excited. Did he make you lick it?"

"No," Christina said in a voice that clearly implied 'yes.'

"So I put this book together, and I made it my finest work. It paints those retreats at Meddleworth House in quite a different light than Donna's starry-eyed history book. We already have a six-figure deal with Red Herring's biggest competitor. When the book comes out, it would have destroyed Hugh's reputation. He'd be dragged through the press and I would have enjoyed every single moment of it." She glared at me. "But then Mina had to go and murder him and ruin my plan."

"I didn't murder him!" I cried. "What reason could I possibly have to kill Hugh?"

"Of all of us, you're the one with the most plausible motive," Killian jumped on. "Hugh's been rubbishing your novel all weekend. If he said those things about Christina's book, I'd want to stab him, too."

"Is that you making a threat?" I tried to deflect attention back to Killian. "You're trying to throw attention on me, but *you're* the one promising violence."

"And the only actual violence we've encountered this weekend was when your boyfriend attacked Hugh!"

"But Heathcliff wasn't in the room with us." An idea occurred to me. "But Oscar was. He was lying at my feet, with no gap between my legs and the coffee table. If I murdered Hugh, I'd have to stand up, get over Oscar, move around the table, find Hugh, and manage to stab him in the neck in the *exact* spot to pierce his artery, in the dark, as a blind woman…"

"You led the way to the door," Donna pointed out.

"*Oscar* led the way," I corrected. "I'm used to not needing my eyes to navigate a room, but I didn't train my guide dog to locate the artery on a man's neck. To kill someone in that way would require a considerable amount of force, and the blow would have to be precise. Otherwise he wouldn't die." I turned to Charlie. "What do your years of experience as a detective say?"

Charlie was probably too stupid to know it, but this was a test. I knew that my guys had inspected the body carefully, and I wanted to make sure they all came to the same conclusions.

"Not necessarily," Charlie said. "My conclusion is that this was a lucky swing from someone who lashed out in anger, taking advantage of the darkness to get their revenge but not intending to kill Hugh…"

"Ah, but you're forgetting another detail," Morrie placed an object on the table. "Hugh Briston's lucky pen."

"That's…the murder weapon? You pulled it out of his neck?"

"I used gloves." Morrie raised his hands to show the white kitchen gloves he'd found. "And I sealed it in a Ziploc bag. The police will still be able to get DNA and fingerprints from it. It's the key to this mystery."

"How so?" Charlie sounded wary.

Morrie leaned back in his chair and steepled his fingers. "I consider myself an expert when it comes to deadly blows. I inspected the wound, and I do not believe Hugh died from blood loss caused by the injury."

That was news to me.

"At first, I thought Hugh had been killed from the pen being shoved in his carotid artery," Morrie began. "But as Mina suggested, that's an incredibly difficult way to kill someone, especially in the dark. It's usually done by dragging a knife across the throat to sever the artery, but this was done by stabbing the pen, which means that the killer would have to be deadly accurate."

"That's right," I jumped in, remembering a discussion about this very subject with Jo and Morrie at the Rose & Wimple one night. "And the more common way to cut someone's throat, according to our friend Jo the medical examiner, is from behind. Even in the dark, Hugh would have noticed someone directly in front of him as they would have blocked the light from the fire, and he seemed like the kind of man to say something, but none of us heard a word. So I think it's safe to assume that the murderer came up behind Hugh. But how would they have known where to stab him? That would require extensive medical training, not to mention sight..."

"Ah, but that's only *if* Hugh was killed by the pen stabbing his carotid artery." Morrie opened the top of the bag containing the pen. "And I don't think that's what happened. There's simply not enough blood. What there is, is the distinct scent of almonds."

"Almonds?" I remembered something else, something from Mrs. Scarlett's murder. "That's cyanide."

"I knew that," Christina said. "The heroine in my first novel kills her husband with a little cyanide mixed into his coffee every morning—"

"That's chronic poisoning, where a little bit of poison builds up in the system over time. What we're talking about here is a lethal dose of poison administered directly into Hugh's bloodstream."

"That's one way to put a stop to the rotten bastard," Vivianne said. "I won't say I'm sad about it, even though it ruins all my plans. I *almost* wish I'd done it myself, although of course, I did not. But how did the cyanide get into Hugh's pen? He never lets that ugly thing out of his sight. Apparently, Stephen King dropped it at a party, back when Hugh was just an editorial intern, and he picked it up and kept it and it's given him good luck ever since. Every book he edits with that pen turns into a bestseller."

"He lost it this afternoon, remember?" My heart raced as the pieces slotted together. "He had it in the morning, but then he was looking for it all afternoon, and this evening it was right back next to his chair. Someone must have stolen it and added the poison in the afternoon, before bringing the pen back and replacing it on Hugh's table."

"And where would they have got the cyanide from?" Vivianne demanded. "That's not something you find lying around."

"They have some in the metalworking workshops," Quoth said. He added quickly, "We took a tour of them before the painting class started. It's used in some metalworking finishes."

"Then that could have been anyone," Killian said. "We're right back where we started."

"I don't think so," Charlie said. "Perhaps you need thirty-three years on the force to see it, but the picture is becoming clearer. The pen went missing after Mina's boyfriend tried to make Hugh choke to death, creating the perfect distraction so Mina could pocket the pen. And we've just established that anyone could have stood behind Hugh and stabbed him with the pen if the only intention was to get the cyanide into his bloodstream."

"But, once again, I still wouldn't have been able to navigate around all over you without Oscar..." I said, but I trailed off as I realized that Charlie was right. In his scenario, I was a plausible suspect.

I realized something else, too.

Heathcliff couldn't have been in the room, but *Quoth* could.

The vent they described wasn't large enough for a human to fit through, but a shapeshifting raven could have flown in and out easily, and no one would have noticed him with the lights out.

But that's absurd. Quoth would never kill someone...

But was it absurd? All my guys had seen how much Hugh upset me. And they made it perfectly clear that they were willing to do anything for me. Even murder.

Donna did find them in the closet together after Heathcliff attacked Hugh. *And* they lied to me about it by saying they only texted each other.

I forgot sometimes that I was dating men who grew up inside storybooks. They were all the villains in their stories – Morrie, the Napoleon of Crime who was responsible for half that is evil and all that is undetected in Sherlock Holmes' London. Heathcliff, the gothic antihero who would orchestrate the downfall of an entire family because he was so broken over Cathy's death. And Quoth, the grim, ungainly, ghastly, gaunt, and ominous bird of yore, an ancient symbol of death and foreboding.

As much as I loved them, they *were* storybook villains. And nothing is off-limits for a villain when the one he loves is threatened.

Did Morrie, Heathcliff, and Quoth get rid of Hugh...for me?

CHAPTER TWENTY

J couldn't say anything about my disturbing thoughts in front of the other writers, who bickered back and forth about the facts of the case, taking it in turns to blame each other until Christina was in tears and Charlie pounded the table so hard it cracked.

I kept trying to catch Heathcliff's eye, certain that with his brutal, bitter honesty, he would be the first to crack.

But it was quite difficult to catch someone's eye when you're blind.

Kelly-Ann, the artist who ran the painting workshops and art studio, poked her head around the door and told Jonathan that the staff had finished serving supper and the guests had been escorted back to their rooms with candles and flashlights. "On the radio, they're saying it could be days until they get through to us. We need to try and get the power back on, but you're the only one who knows how to operate the generator."

"I have to guard these miscreants," Jonathan said.

"We'll take over for a bit." Kelly-Ann stepped into the room, and I saw a couple of cleaners and chefs behind her. "We may not have the brawn, but several of us should be fine to guard them for a bit."

"Fine." Jonathan stood and pointed at Heathcliff, Morrie, and Quoth. "I'll take those three with me, and *you*," he nodded at Donna and Christina. "You can come too and go to the bathroom since you're so desperate."

Morrie kissed me on the head as he got up to leave. "Don't you worry, gorgeous. Things will be back to normal in no time. We've almost cracked this case."

Yes, I thought glumly. *That might well be true. But I don't know if I want to know the answer.*

The staff poured in. They carried a couple of supper trays with some cold meats, cheese, crackers, relish, and some slices of Victoria sponge cake. I had to ask one of the staff members if they could get me some cheese and crackers, since I couldn't see to do it myself in the dark without getting my fingers all over the food.

"I'll do that for you." Kelly-Ann cut a few slabs of cheese, adding dabs of relish and plonking them down on a plate in front of me. I fed a piece of cold roast beef to Oscar under the table. He'd been such a good boy all evening.

"You're the art teacher?" I asked her.

"Yes. I'm not really supposed to talk to you." She wiggled further away from me. "You could be the murderer."

"I promise that I'm not. But I understand that you're afraid, and I won't come any closer. I just wanted to tell you that I saw one of your paintings in our room. I can't see a lot these days, but your work – especially your use of color – is so bold and vivid that it stood out to me."

"Thank you."

"Allan's enjoying working with you," I smiled, even though my heart was hammering in my chest.

"Allan?"

"Yeah, my friend Allan. He's the guy with the long, silky black hair. He's taking your art class. He had to miss the afternoon session because...I needed him, but he was in the studio this evening when the power went out."

"Nope. I don't know who that is. I only have three students in the class. I remember them all, and he isn't one of them." Kelly-Ann shook her head. "There was another person who signed up for the class, but he never showed up. That's pretty common. I've been in the studio all evening, and I never saw that guy."

Panic crept along my spine. "And there's not another painting studio? Like, a small one where someone could work and you wouldn't see?"

"Nope. Not unless you're talking about the metalworking studio or the pottery suite."

"But..." It didn't make sense. Quoth left for the art class this morning. He came back in his paint-splattered work clothes.

Quoth would never lie to me. *Never.*

Except that he already had once today.

Another memory assailed me – Quoth flying in the window of our room after Morrie told him about what Hugh said about me. A shiny object dangled from his beak.

Hugh's pen.

It had to be. It was pen-shaped.

Why did Quoth have it?

Why wasn't he where he said he was when the power went out?

What is going on?

CHAPTER TWENTY-ONE

Bree: Mina, I know it's the middle of the night and you might not see this, but just letting you know that I'm taking Grimalkin to the all-night vet in Grimdale. She's still not eating or moving much, and she has some strange discharge. We're in a taxi now.

Pax is singing songs about slaying druids to her and that seems to be keeping her calm.

You're jumping to conclusions, I told myself as I polished off the rest of my hot chocolate and licked relish off my fingers. *You don't know for a fact that the object in Quoth's beak was the pen. And even if it was, they couldn't have pulled together this elaborate murder plot, because they wouldn't be able to predict that the power would go off.*

Actually, that was the only flaw in our current theory – to pull off this murder inside the locked room, the killer had to do the deed in the dark. Which means that they had to know the power would go off. But no one could predict the storm…

The door banged, and Heathcliff stepped through the door,

followed by Morrie and Quoth, and finally Christina, who sighed with relief. She must have been to the bathroom.

My stomach churned as Heathcliff sat down next to me, the belt of his robe brushing my thigh. I had to find out the truth. But how? If my guys did set this up to frame one of the writers in the room, they did an amazing job.

"Hey." Charlie ran his hands across the table. "The pen is gone. Someone has destroyed the one piece of evidence that might identify the killer—"

"We placed it back in the library," Heathcliff said. "I didn't want it here where grubby fingers might contaminate it."

"And where are Jonathan and Donna?" demanded Charlie.

"Donna's in the bathroom, and Jonathan is out in the maintenance shed, trying to sort out the mess," Heathcliff said, his voice grim. "The power isn't out because of the storm. Someone cut the lines. Jonathan is trying to rig up the generator now, but he sent us back here to guard you all. Someone wanted Meddleworth House in the dark."

CHAPTER TWENTY-TWO

"This is absurd." Vivianne stood up as Morrie shooed out the hotel staff. "It was one thing when Jonathan was guarding us, but it's quite another for one of the suspect's boyfriends to be in charge. If one of the people in this room is a murderer, then they must have had an accomplice outside the room to turn off the power. Anyone in this hotel could be in on it, and I for one will not be a sitting duck! I'm leaving."

She stalked toward the door. To my shock, Heathcliff stepped aside and let her through.

"Anyone else want to run?" he boomed. "Now's your chance."

"Hey, wait a second." I tugged on his arm as the rest of the writers filed past us and disappeared into the hotel. "How could you let everyone leave? We can't have the murderer running loose around the hotel."

"That's exactly what we want," Heathcliff growled.

"Why don't you stop him?" I glared at Morrie and Quoth as I shook Heathcliff's arm. "What are you doing?"

"We're solving the murder, of course." Heathcliff folded his arms. "No need to thank me."

"I don't understand. You let all the suspects go!"

Unless, of course, you know that none of them are suspects.

"I told all the suspects that I put the pen back in the library. That pen contains DNA evidence the police need to convict our killer. Whoever is responsible is not going to pass up the opportunity to sneak back to the library, steal it, and get rid of it. And when they do, we're going to catch them."

I gaped at him. "You...you set up a trap? That's dangerous. What if the murderer goes upstairs and hurts one of the guests?"

"Relax, gorgeous," Morrie said. "I know murderers, and ours set this up deliberately and carefully to ensure they got away with it. They won't waste the opportunity to get rid of the pen."

"Morrie and I are going after them." Heathcliff walked across the room to a coat of arms and yanked two ancient swords from the display. He tossed one to Morrie, who caught it with the grace of a championship fencer. "We need to leave now if we want to surprise them. You stay here with Quoth. I don't want you anywhere near the murderer."

I was too flabbergasted and incensed to reply. The room fell silent as they shut the door behind them, leaving me and Quoth alone in the gloom.

The candles on the table flickered, casting eerie shadows over Quoth's waterfall of dark hair.

"Are you okay?" he asked in that kind, husky voice of his. "It can't be nice being accused of murder, especially since this isn't the first time. But if Heathcliff and Morrie can catch the real killer, they will clear your name."

"The other writers have every right to accuse me," I said. "My motive is at least as strong as everyone else's. Hugh was a pretty rotten guy."

"I don't think anyone will cry over his death."

"No, but just because someone is awful doesn't mean killing them is a just thing to do. Don't you agree?"

Was it my imagination, or did Quoth stiffen a little beside me? "Of course. Is there any cheese left?"

"Quoth…" I sighed. I needed to know the truth, and I knew I'd be able to make Quoth give it to me. "I know you didn't go to art class today."

He froze, his hand hovering over the platter.

"I talked to Kelly-Ann, and she said you never showed up." I tried to touch his hand, but he angled himself away from me. "Where were you? Why did you lie to me?"

He slumped down, his hair falling over his face, a curtain hiding his eyes. "I was embarrassed. I'm sorry, Mina. I went to speak to the ravens again. I'm trying to figure out a way to free them. I asked Donna about them, but she said that people didn't want them hopping around the tables while they were eating—"

Quoth's words were cut off by a shrill shriek.

"That's someone screaming," I said, leaping to my feet. "The murderer is striking again!"

CHAPTER TWENTY-THREE

*W*e followed the screams into the hallway, but from there they cut off abruptly, and I didn't know which way to go.

"Let's check the library." Quoth's voice thickened with worry.

We raced along the winding corridor. Oscar's toenails clacked against the tiles, matching the pounding of my heart. Quoth shoved open the library door. The fire had burned down to embers now, which thankfully meant I could barely see Hugh's dead body slumped beside it. The room appeared empty, but I knew better.

"What happened?" I cried. "Who did you kill now?"

"What are you talking about?" Heathcliff growled from a not-so-subtle hiding spot behind the curtains.

"No one's come into the room," Morrie unfolded his long body from behind the cuckoo clock and crossed in front of the fire. "And what do you mean, who did we kill *now*?"

I ignored his question. "So the scream didn't come from this room?"

"Nope. It must have been the other end of the house, or outside."

"Mina, are you okay?" Quoth squeezed my hand.

Cold determination settled inside me. *I have to find out the truth, even if it's what I don't want to hear.*

I crossed the room and slammed the door shut. "We need to talk."

CHAPTER TWENTY-FOUR

*Q*uoth took my hand and pulled me and Oscar across the room, moving all of us closer to the fire where he knew I could see a little. He leaned in close, his face shadowed with worry. "Mina, what's this about?"

"It's about…" I swallowed. "You. Us. What's been going on this weekend."

"If you're referring to what Heathcliff and I got up to this morning, we would have happily invited you, gorgeous, but you were off with the birdie—"

"No, it's not about that." I squeezed my eyes shut. I couldn't bear to look at them. "I've been putting the clues together, and… it all adds up."

"What adds up?" Quoth squeezed my fingers so tight it hurt a little. "Mina, you're scaring me."

"Just tell me one thing…what you were talking about when Donna caught the three of you whispering together in the laundry closet? Tell me what you were discussing, and I'll go back to my hiding place and let you get on with catching the murderer."

No one spoke. My stomach churned. I opened one eye. Lightning forked through the sky outside, and I could just see the three of them exchanging a long, meaningful look with each other.

"What do you think we were doing?" said Heathcliff in a slightly accusing tone. "We were discussing my outburst. Morrie was recommending me some anger management courses."

"I know an excellent fellow in London," Morrie said. "He was wonderful to talk to after I first came into this world with an insatiable thirst for revenge."

Their words sounded so plausible. But I knew better. Heathcliff would *never* talk about his anger issues, *especially* not with Morrie. He didn't regret hurting Hugh, because Hugh had hurt me and Heathcliff would never stand for that. He had real 'touch her and die' dark romance hero energy.

Which was what had led us to this point in the first place. 'Touch her and die' might be a fun, sexy trope for a romance novel, but in real life, it was crazy and creepy and *illegal*.

"That's a lie, and you know it. The three of you conspired to kill Hugh, didn't you?"

"Wh-wh-what?" Quoth stammered.

"Oh, gorgeous." Morrie's lips curled back into his signature smirk.

"You think we murdered that bastard?" Heathcliff glowered.

He whirled around and stuck his sword into the wall. It stuck out, the thin blade wobbling. Heathcliff's shoulders heaved with distress.

"Isn't that what you were threatening to do? Isn't that why you're all hiding in the library right now, and why you destroyed the pen under the guise of catching the killer? You're trying to figure out how to cover up what you did, how to frame one of the other writers for it."

I squeezed my eyes shut again. I couldn't bear to stare into Quoth's eyes while I talked about this. I didn't believe it. I couldn't. And yet...

I had to be strong. I had to go with what the evidence said.

"You already didn't like Hugh because of what he said to me at the opening ceremony. Maybe you even planned some kind of trick to get back at him then. But then Heathcliff overheard Hugh in the library, and he flew into a rage. When you realized that you couldn't kill him in front of all those witnesses, the three of you had your secret meeting and decided to get your revenge on Hugh."

"Go on, gorgeous," Morrie purred. "I'm intrigued to hear how we masterminded murdering someone from the outside of a locked room."

"It's quite brilliant, really. I wouldn't expect anything less from you three. First, you all went upstairs one at a time and told me the story about texting each other so I wouldn't incriminate you. Then, you had Quoth steal Hugh's pen, which he had in his mouth when he arrived at our room. That's what he was talking about before he saw me. 'After everything I went through to get it.' That's what you said, wasn't it?" I turned to Quoth.

"Yes," he said miserably.

"And then, Heathcliff and Morrie pretended to go to the spa, while Quoth stayed with me. Only, when you went out to get me some snacks, you actually met the others, where Morrie handed you back the pen that he'd filled with cyanide from the supply in the blacksmith's forge. You knew from Jonathan's weather reports that the storm would get worse, and Donna had told you that the sessions would be conducted in a locked room from now on. So you waited until all the writers were gathered for the evening critique session, then Heathcliff or Morrie disabled the power while Quoth flew in through the heating vent, did the deed with the pen, and disappeared back through the vent before anyone noticed. You knew that there was no way the police would be able to convict you because there is absolutely no way another human could get into and out of this room, and you probably figured they'd be unlikely to consider the blind girl a suspect. And it's brilliant, it truly is, and I'm so grateful you feel that way about me, but you *murdered* someone. Didn't you? Please tell me I'm wrong."

No one spoke.

"Well." I glared at each of them in turn. "Stay something!"

Morrie dropped his sword on the rug.

He burst out laughing.

"I don't think this is funny," Heathcliff said. "Mina suspects us capable of murder."

"Of course she does. Mina's no fool. She's put every clue together and come up with the most logical explanation. And she knows us better than anyone, better even than we know ourselves. She has loved us in books long before she loved us in real life. I *am* the Napoleon of Crime. Quoth is a portent of death. And you...you who were driven mad once by your love, can you honestly say that you would not kill for this woman?" Morrie touched my shoulder with such surprising tenderness that my heart broke a little. He continued to admonish Heathcliff. "When you barged into this room the other day, wasn't your intention to shove Hugh Briston's head into the fire and relish his screams? I have read your novel, and it was always ambiguous whether or not you killed Hindley—"

"Stop." I held up my hand. I didn't want to hear any more. Tears streamed down my cheeks. "I need the truth. Did you do this thing? Did you murder for me?"

Quoth reached out to me, his fingers hanging in the air, hesitant, unsure if I wanted his touch. I didn't know myself.

"Of course we did not," he whispered. "Morrie is right. We each of us would kill for you. But you didn't need us to kill for you. You were so determined to handle Hugh on your own, Mina. You're so strong, you don't need us to swoop in like dark knights and make your problems go away."

I sniffed. Relief welled up inside me and flooded me. The tears came thick and fast. They didn't do it. They didn't kill Hugh.

Then why the secret meeting in the laundry closet, and the object in Quoth's mouth—

"But you are right." Quoth's fire-rimmed eyes bore into mine. "We have been hiding something from you."

"We should have known better than to try and keep a secret from you," Morrie added.

My heart hammered. "What secret?"

Quoth stepped back. He exchanged a look with the other two, a wordless conversation passing between them.

Morrie nodded.

Heathcliff nodded.

What's going on?

Quoth pulled something out of his pocket.

All three of them fell on one knee around me.

My stomach dropped into my toes.

"Mina." Quoth clasped my hand in his, bringing it to his face but not kissing it. His fingers trembled beneath mine. Morrie and Heathcliff each placed a hand on top of his, and the three of them gazed up at me with so much love and hope and adoration that I lost the ability to speak. "Will you marry us?"

CHAPTER TWENTY-FIVE

*O*h.
      My.

Isis.

They're proposing.

They're proposing to me.

With his free hand, Quoth pulled something from his pocket and dropped it into my hand. It was a shimmering gold velvet drawstring bag. "Open it," he urged. "It's what I was storing in the safe in our room and carrying in my beak today. I finished it just before the murder."

I dropped Oscar's harness and dug my fingers into the bag, tipping out a metal object into my palm.

A ring.

A *ring.*

I held it up to the firelight and ran my fingers over it, enjoying the twisted metal band and the different textures. Four glittering stones were set into it, like fruits hanging from the branches of a gnarled tree.

"What…what is this?"

"I thought it was obvious. It's your engagement ring. I took the stones that Morrie had and made this." Quoth grinned shyly. "When I saw in the Meddleworth brochure that they had a jewelry-making course, I had the idea and told Heathcliff and Morrie. That's why Kelly-Ann hadn't seen me at the painting studio – I told you I signed up for a painting class, but I've really been over in the forge, making this."

My breath hitched as I touched each jewel in turn. A rare orange diamond that glistened with fire where the light caught it, just like Quoth's eyes. A sapphire as cold and clear as ice for Morrie, and an onyx as deep and black and mesmerizing as Heathcliff. And for me, a brilliant emerald – the facets dancing in the firelight and creating rainbow prisms across my skin.

"We've been thinking about this for a long time." Lightning cracked, illuminating the edges of Heathcliff's dark eyes as they burned into mine. "But every time we thought we came up with a plan, your mother would interrupt with one of her schemes or Mrs. Ellis would need some help at the village bingo night or someone would get murdered or a mischievous Shakespearean fairy would steal your slippers."

"When you were invited to Meddleworth and you were so excited about your writing, we thought this would be the perfect chance...away from Argleton and the shop and all the murders," Morrie said with a laugh. "Of course, it was wistful thinking to hope that a murder wouldn't follow us."

"But in a way, it's perfect," Quoth said.

"Very on-brand," Heathcliff added with a tiny, beautiful smile.

"But..." I turned the ring over and over. It was absolutely perfect. "But we can't get married...legally, I mean..."

"I said before, no puritanical marriage law will keep us apart," Morrie said. "The four of us are written in the stars."

"Mina Wilde doesn't do things the normal way," Heathcliff added. "And she especially doesn't do things the *legal* way. Not when love is at stake."

"We're all ready to make some kind of wild, zany, rock 'n' roll, proclamation to the world," Quoth said. "What do you think?"

I studied each of them in turn. Heathcliff with his enormous shoulders hunched nervously. Quoth's lip quirked into a heart-melting question. Morrie played with a loose thread in his cuff, his usual smirk gone. Instead, he chewed on his lower lip.

He was nervous.

James Moriarty – the spider at the center of a vast criminal web, the greatest criminal mastermind ever written – was *nervous*.

"Well?" Heathcliff demanded, his voice a storm of emotion. "Will you?"

"Will I?"

"Will you make us the happiest men in this world and in all worlds that the great writers of this age could possibly invent, and marry us, Mina Wilde?"

CHAPTER TWENTY-SIX

My eyes fluttered shut. I needed a moment where I wasn't looking at their expectant faces, where I could rest within the stillness of the gloom and ask myself if I wanted this.

I loved them so much that it hurt, but this...this was a big, bold commitment. This was *forever*.

I closed my fingers around the ring.

I drew a deep breath.

I opened my eyes.

"I would love to be your wife."

"Oh, thank fuck," Heathcliff breathed.

Quoth's fingers trembled as he slid the ring onto my finger. It fit perfectly. I held it up, turning it this way and that, admiring the way the gems sparkled. One for each of us, but they all fit together to create a whole.

"Morrie wanted me to make four matching rings," Quoth said. "But I decided that all the stones should be in your ring because you are our center. Nevermore Bookshop may have made us corporeal, but when you came along, you gave us something to live for. You have our hearts, Mina, and we'll spend every moment of every day treating you like the heroine of a romance novel."

Tears rolled down my cheeks.

I leaned forward and wrapped my arms around Quoth's neck. He pulled me in close, his long fingers skimming my sides before gripping my hips. "And you have my heart," I whispered. "Always and forever."

He kissed me with all the tender love that Poe wrote about so achingly. He kissed me like a windswept beach and a crumbling house on a cliff, like all the dark beautiful things that joined our souls.

When Quoth drew away, his face lit up with a smile so pure and adoring.

I hadn't seen him smile like that in a long, long time.

A strong hand drew around my waist. Quoth stepped away as Morrie spun me around, my chest meeting his. His intense icicle eyes bore into mine, glinting with shattered light from the lightning crackling outside. "You're sure you're not making a big mistake, gorgeous? No one has loved Moriarty and lived to tell the tale."

"Sure they have," I grinned back. "Sherlock lives in a flat above a fish and chip shop in Chelsea."

Morrie gave a dark chuckle. He leaned forward and touched my lips with a feathery kiss that stole my breath and promised oh so much more mischief to come.

Heathcliff shoved Morrie out of the way and wrapped his strong arms around me. His lips met mine, sweeping me away with the sheer possessive force of his love.

I knew beyond all realms of knowing that I had made the right decision. I wanted this, right here, with the three of them, for the rest of my life.

Heathcliff's kiss deepened, going from possessive to desperate in moments. He backed me up against the wall. His tongue thrust between my lips, devouring me, making me his.

"What do you say?" he growled. "Should the three of us make our fiancée scream her pleasure into this bitter, beautiful storm?"

"In the library? Anyone could come in and see us. Didn't you set up this trap for the murderer?"

"We could lock the door." Morrie appeared at Heathcliff's side in a flash. "After all, the culprit hasn't shown up yet. Maybe they've been cornered by Charlie and are being forced to listen to the story of every murder he's solved in thirty-three years on the force."

"But what about, uh, Hugh Briston's corpse..."

"We'll make you forget all about him." Morrie knelt on the carpet in front of me. Heathcliff moved back a bit, his arms still tight around me, as Morrie's long fingers made short work of the buttons on my slacks. I fumbled for the belt on Heathcliff's robe, sliding it open stroking my fiancé's length through his boxers.

My fiancés. I will never get tired of saying that.

Morrie made a delighted sound as he pulled my panties to the side. His tongue slid between my legs, and Isis damn him, but he was right. This was what being engaged to three villains did to you. I knew that Hugh was *right there,* but I couldn't think about anything except for the pleasure rushing through my veins and the fact that the men with their tongues down my throat and between my legs would be my husbands...

I cried out as the wall gave way behind me, and we toppled backward into the gloom.

CHAPTER TWENTY-SEVEN

"*A*rgh!" I cried out as my back slammed into the hard floor.

Heathcliff cursed as he came down on top of me, his bulk driving the wind from my lungs.

"Are you okay?" He helped me to my knees, rubbing circles on my back as I coughed.

"I think I swallowed my tongue…" I reached out a hand, and Heathcliff and Morrie helped me to my feet. "I'm okay. What happened?"

"Heathcliff was hogging our fiancée, so I'd just plunged my tongue inside you to stake my own claim," Morrie said. "when the wall gave way behind you."

That explains how I fell backward, but I don't understand how a solid wall could just give way like that…

I glanced at the wall, but all I could see was a dark rectangle where the wooden panels and a boring painting of a sailboat once were. Quoth slipped inside the gloom, then came back out again.

"It's a secret passage," he said, his voice grave. "The wall is spring loaded. It extends through the wall here and around the corner. There's another spring on the other end – I think the door will open out into the hallway that leads out to the kitchen, but it seems to be locked on the other side. It's quite wide, wider than you'd expect for a secret passage—"

"I know what that is," Morrie said. "It's a servants' passage."

"A what?"

"In old houses like this, these types of passages were installed so that the staff could move in and out of the rooms without having to pass the guests in the halls. It's wide so the kitchen staff could carry trays of food into this room without going the long way around and carrying them past guests mingling in the hallway."

"It's kind of cool." Quoth disappeared inside again.

"It's also an important clue," I said, my heart hammering. "If this passage leads outside, it means that someone else could have snuck into the room and killed Hugh."

CHAPTER TWENTY-EIGHT

$\mathcal{W}$e gathered around the entrance to the servants' passage and contemplated the meaning of this new discovery.

"Every part of our investigation so far was built on the assumption that only the writers within the room could have committed the crime." Morrie said in his 'I'm thinking deep thoughts' voice. I couldn't see him, but I knew he'd be rubbing his chin. "We never considered how someone from outside could get in and out again without anyone seeing."

"Mina considered it," Heathcliff reminded him, but there was no hint of anger in his voice. "She thought *we* did it."

"Mina is cleverer than the rest of us. This passage opens up a whole new host of possibilities. Any one of the staff or guests at the lodge could have done the deed."

"But who?" Quoth asked. "Does anyone on the staff have a motive for killing Hugh?"

"He's been coming to the castle for years for these sodding retreats," Heathcliff said. "He's bound to put someone's back up with his charming personality."

"He's a tosser, but you don't kill people for being unpleasant,"

Morrie said. "Well, most people don't. I've definitely fallen off that particular bandwagon from time to time."

"It's unlikely that a guest knew about this doorway," I said. "In fact, it's strange that Donna never mentioned it, since she owns the castle. If she'd told us about the doorway, then we wouldn't have been looking at her as a suspect."

"Maybe she didn't know about it," Quoth said. "She left the house for London the first chance she got. Apart from some scuffed prints on the floor, it's pretty dusty in the tunnel. I don't think people have used it for decades, which means whoever knew about it was familiar with the castle's history…"

Oh Hathor, oh no…

The clues rearranged themselves in my brain, shifting to fit around my horrible theory. I turned to the guys, who were still considering the suspects.

"Donna wrote that book on Meddleworth's history!" Heathcliff said. "She had to know about it."

"I don't think it was her," Morrie said. "It has to be another staff member, someone who would know secrets like this about the castle…"

"We know that Hugh has a thing for young women," Quoth pointed out. "Perhaps he tried something with one of the cleaners or the kitchen staff members, and she decided to teach him a lesson?"

"I know who did it." I turned back to the guys. "I know who the murderer is. It's been staring us in the face the entire time. It's Jonathan."

CHAPTER TWENTY-NINE

t has to be. It all fits.

The more I considered it, the more sure I was that I had the villain.

"How did you figure that out, gorgeous?" Morrie asked, his voice thick with awe.

"Jonathan must have taken the pen when he came in to pull Heathcliff off Hugh," I explained. "In the chaos, he could have pocketed the pen without anyone noticing. He filled it with cyanide from the supply in the forge. He'd know exactly where it was kept. Then, later, he cut the power, came through the passage, struck Hugh in the throat with the pen, and escaped without any of us noticing him in the gloom."

"But Jonathan was trying to get the door open," Morrie said. "You heard him banging on it."

"No. I heard *Fergus* banging on it," I explained, my voice breathless with excitement. This bit really was quite clever. "When I went to the bathroom at the opening drinks, Fergus was throwing his weight against the door. He heard Oscar in the stall with me and he wanted to get to the other dog. Inside the stall, it sounded like someone trying to break down the door. Jonathan must have shut off the power, come back inside with Fergus, and after his initial words to me, he left Fergus to throw himself against the door while he snuck through the butler's passage and killed Hugh."

"Everything about that fits, gorgeous," Morrie said. "Except for one thing. Motive. What possible reason would Jonathan have for killing Hugh?"

"I'm still figuring that out," I said. "But I think it has something to do with the history of the castle that Donna has written. By her own admission, Donna hardly spent any time at the castle. She didn't care about the writers in her parents' circle. She was down in London. But Jonathan has worked here most of his life, and he loves this castle. Think of how many stories he's told us while we were here. I think he might be the real author of the book, but I don't understand why—"

"Well done, Mina Wilde."

I gasped as a shadowy figure appeared in the secret passage. Jonathan. And Fergus was by his side, growling. Jonathan had something huge and heavy in his arms. He stepped into the room and closed the door behind him. "I wondered if you'd figure it out."

CHAPTER THIRTY

*J*onathan lurched toward us. Instinctively, I shrank away from him, pressing my back into Heathcliff's chest.

THUD.

The heavy object dropped from Jonathan's arms onto the floor. Morrie rushed forward, no doubt going for his sword since Heathcliff's was stuck in the wall and now useless.

His body stiffened as he regarded the object in Jonathan's hands.

"This is Donna." Morrie's voice remained steady. "Is she dead? There's blood on her face. What have you done to her?"

"Don't come any closer." Jonathan raised his arm. Morrie froze. "Get back beside the others."

"Mina, he's holding a gun." Morrie backed away to stand in front of us, his body shielding mine and Heathcliff. "And he's just dropped Donna's body on the floor. I can't tell if she's alive or not."

"She's still alive," Jonathan said. "For now. All of you, move to the center of the room, closer to Hugh."

Heathcliff growled low in his throat as he reached down and

tugged the edges of his robe together so they wouldn't flap open. It would've been hilarious if not for how terrified I was. Even though I couldn't see the gun, I could sense it, the coldness of the barrel sucking all the life from the room.

"I knew from the moment I met ye that ye were a clever lass, Mina Wilde," Jonathan said as he moved back toward the passage with Fergus in tow. "I didn't want to have to hurt ye. If you'd just stayed in the dining room, then everything would be okay. But you had to go and discover the passage and ruin everything."

"Jonathan, I don't know what's going on," I said. "But I think I understand a little. You wrote the manuscript that Donna was passing off as her own. That was *your* story. Your love letter to Meddleworth House."

"Aye. It was my father's book. When he worked here, he was looking at the history books in the library, filling in the details to build a history for the house and grounds. I've been adding to his stories, checking facts, compiling dates and names. I've worked on that manuscript every spare moment when I'm not running about after ungrateful guests." He made a rude gesture at Hugh's body still slumped forward in his chair. "The annual writer's retreat was the absolute worst. All these intellectual snobs talking out of their arses and Hugh Briston lording it over all of us while he felt up the maids in the supply closet. I wanted to publish a *real* book – a piece of history so that people could finally see that this house meant something, that it should be preserved and celebrated, instead of used as a den of sin or a *spa*." He spat the word.

"To be fair, the mud wrap is exquisite," Morrie said.

"Not helping," Heathcliff hissed.

"I hand-wrote that manuscript, every last word, fact-checked and sourced with the castle's library. Last year, while Hugh was setting up for his first lecture, I snuck in and told him about it. I said he might like to look at it if he wanted a real story for his publishing company. And do you know what that bastard did?"

Jonathan's voice was as stormy as the wind howling outside. "He laughed. He laughed in my face."

Fergus growled again, sensing his owner's anger.

"He told me that he didn't even have to look at the book to know that there was no way he'd want to publish it. He said that no one cared about a pile of stones in the middle of nowhere."

"I was so upset that I threw the manuscript in the trash. But then I went online and I heard about this thing called self-publishing, where I could get the book edited professionally and then publish it myself. So I thought I'd give that a go. Maybe it wouldn't be a bestseller, but I could offer copies to the guests and maybe make a few bob for my retirement. But when I went to collect the manuscript, it had disappeared. I didn't have a copy, and I thought it was gone forever, but then Donna announced that she'd written a book. It was my book, only she'd taken out chapters of history and replaced them with silly stories about writers and ghosts. And now that there's a pretty lass attached to it, Hugh Briston wants to publish it. But how did you figure it out?"

"I'm also interested," Morrie said. "That was one hell of a guess, gorgeous."

"It wasn't a guess," I said. "I finally figured out something that was niggling at me. Donna gave me a couple of chapters to read. I noticed that the same types of errors kept popping up in her manuscript – for example, the word 'prick' instead of 'pink.' Those errors happen because she had to use OCR scanning software to get the book into a digital format. It scans the hand-writing and tries to guess the letters to create a digital file. I have to use software like that sometimes to scan documents so I can read them on my Braille note. They often get the same letters wrong."

"That's right. Clever girl to spot that," Jonathan said. "By the time I found out that Donna must've been the one who took my manuscript, she already filled it with salacious stories from her childhood and the writer's events and made the deal with Hugh. I confronted her about it, but she said that if I ever breathed a word to anyone, she would fire me and I'd never be able to set foot onto the Meddleworth estate ever again." His voice trembled with emotion. "My da is buried here, in a grave on top of the ridge. I can't leave him. I can't leave this place. She had no right to take that away from me."

"So why kill Hugh?" Quoth asked. "Donna was the one who stole your manuscript."

Jonathan snorted. "Hugh had no respect for Meddleworth. He treated it like his personal playground. And he wouldn't even look at the book when I handed it to him, but he saw a pretty skirt and changed his tune. He had to go. I thought I'd come up with the perfect plan – kill Hugh and ruin Donna's plans for making her millions off the book. None of her fancy London toffs would want to come to a spa where someone had been brutally murdered. No, Donna would be forced to leave Meddleworth in the hands of someone who knew how to take care of it."

"Someone like you," I breathed.

"Aye. I would give this castle the care she deserves. I'll tear out the poxy spa and free the ravens and make the grounds beautiful again. So I came up with my plan. The storm gave me the perfect excuse, and when Donna announced she was going to lock the room, it made everything even more perfect. Hugh Briston had bespoiled the name of Meddleworth, and he had to die. You should have seen his face when I stepped in front of him. He was so surprised."

Donna groaned.

My heart raced. *At least she's alive.*

But for how long?

What are we going to do?

Every plan I came up with fell apart with the gun pointed at us.

Is this where we all die?

Jonathan continued. "And one of the writers would be framed for his murder. I didn't much care who. They're all the same, coming here every year with their airs and desperation, clinging to every word that awful man said like he was a god, treating me and the other staff like we couldn't possibly understand their lofty literary conversations.

"But then you all decided to play detective. And at first, it was going smoothly, all the writers bickering and blaming each other, as I knew they would do. But then I realized that you were getting closer to figuring things out. I didn't plan for Mina Wilde and her three boyfriends to solve the crime. Silly Fergus gave me away." He stepped over Donna's prone body and advanced on us. "But now, that leaves me with a problem. What exactly am I to do with the four of you?"

CHAPTER THIRTY-ONE

"You're not doing anything," Heathcliff growled. He and Morrie surged forward, aiming for Jonathan, hoping their combined bulk would take the murderer by surprise.

"No," I cried out. One of them would be shot—

But, to my shock, Jonathan didn't fire. Instead, he darted across the room and out the main door. Fergus whimpered as he was dragged along behind him. Heathcliff lunged at the door, but Jonathan slammed it shut behind him. I heard a click and knew that he'd locked it from the other side.

"Sorry to do this to such lovely people," he yelled through the wall, and I thought he really was sorry. "But I can't have you blabbing to the police. It all has to be neat and tidy, you see."

Heathcliff banged his fist on the door. "You let us out of this room this instant!"

"No can do, I'm afraid. You can rage all you like, but in a few minutes, you won't feel a thing."

My blood stilled in my veins.

What's he talking about?

"Don't worry, it's a peaceful way to go. I've redirected natural gas from the heating into the old vents in this room. It's a common issue in old houses like this – a gas leak goes undetected until someone locks a door. I've sealed the secret passage shut, so you can't escape there. By the time the police arrive at the castle, it will be too late for all of you."

CHAPTER THIRTY-TWO

"*H*e's going to gas us!" I gasped.

Warm arms went around me as Morrie pulled me into his chest. Heathcliff hammered on the door, yelling for one of the guests or staff to let us out, but I'm guessing that Jonathan found a way to keep them all away from this part of the castle.

I don't want to go out like this. I don't want to die.

"Donna, can you hear me?" Quoth bent over her prone body, trying to rouse her. "It's no good. She's not waking up."

In the hallway, Jonathan whistled, and I could hear Fergus barking as Jonathan dragged him away.

My lungs contracted. How long had Jonathan been pumping natural gas into the room? He probably turned it on the moment he got outside. Maybe even before.

How long did we have left?

Heathcliff moved to the windows, slamming his fist into the glass. "Some bastard has covered the glass in security bars," he growled. "We're not getting out through here."

Morrie pulled me across the room. He tried to get the secret passage to open again, but whatever Jonathan had done to it, it was sealed shut. He picked up his sword from where he'd discarded it on the rug. "I can try using this to smash through the wall, but we don't have much time."

"I vote for smashing."

Morrie swung his sword at the wall. I coughed as plaster dust went up my nose. Or was it my airways filling with the gas?

Crockery and pastries crashed to the floor as Heathcliff flung the remains of the snack buffet off the table. He hoisted the heavy wooden table off the ground and flung it at the main door. Wood cracked and splintered, but no escape appeared.

My head felt impossibly light, as if it was floating off my neck and away from my body. Morrie discarded his sword, grabbed a statue from a nearby sconce, and hurled it at the wall. But he was moving too slow, his limbs swimming through air made of golden syrup. Everything was too slow.

I tried to speak, but the words felt like wet spaghetti, slipping through my fingers.

Quoth dropped Donna's hand. "Mina..." he gasped out. "I can't breathe..."

Quoth. My beautiful Quoth. I couldn't believe I thought he was a murderer, just because he was the only one who could fit through...

Oh, shit. The vent...

"Quoth..." I tried to get my brain to send a message to my mouth, but it took an age before I could make my lips form the words. "You have to fly out the vent."

"Vent?"

"The vent. The one you found. It's up there." I managed to lift my hand and point a shaking finger at the square on the top of the wall. "Fly out. Get help."

Quoth transformed in impossibly slow motion and flew toward the vent high on the wall, but he was affected even worse by the gas as a small raven, and the gas would be rising to the top of the room. It took him four attempts before he could fly high enough to reach the grate. He dug his beak into the grate and tried to unclip it, but his flying was erratic. He kept slipping.

I can't...I'm getting so tired... Quoth's voice croaked inside my head.

"I'll help...birdie..." Heathcliff grabbed the edge of the table and hauled himself to his feet. He staggered across the room just as Quoth started to slip down the wall, his talons scrabbling to maintain a hold on the grate.

With a last surge of effort, Heathcliff reached the wall. He grabbed the statue from Morrie and swung. Quoth darted out of the way, dropping back to land on the table. The statue struck the grate, knocking out the clip. I heard a clatter as the metal grate hit the floor.

"Hurry..." I gasped.

Quoth spread his midnight wings and soared upward. At the last second, he tucked his wings into his body and dove through the vent. I couldn't see him after that.

Heathcliff dropped to his knees. His knuckles dragged on the ground as he collapsed on the floor.

"I've got you, big guy..." Morrie crawled over. He lay down beside Heathcliff, wrapping his arms around him. He grunted, and I realized he was trying to drag Heathcliff's bulk across the rug to me. "We're coming, gorgeous..."

With a last burst of energy, I hauled myself across the floor toward them. Morrie's arm fell over my shoulder, pulling me into them both. Everything felt far away and unimportant. It didn't seem so bad to just close my eyes and...

CRASH.

I was dimly aware that somewhere far away, the world was tearing apart. I snuggled in deeper, sinking into the warmth of Morrie and Heathcliff as we drew our last breath together...

SMASH RIIIIIIIP

Bright lights danced across my eyes.

This is it. This is the end.

At least I've had a good life. I followed my dreams, tried to be nice to people, ate a lot of pastries, and had tons of sex with fictional villains.

"Mina..." Morrie whispered. "Look."

I don't want to look. I want to go to sleep.

A finger pressed into the back of my neck, jabbing me insistently.

Fine, fine, I'll look, but then you have to let me die in peace...

It took everything I had left to open my eyes. I stared into a pair of blinding lights. Maybe we were already dead? But I'd already technically died once, and it was much more watery than this. My friend Bree, who can do some interesting things with ghosts, said that when you die you see one light. Why did I see two? And they were growing larger as they got closer and closer and...

HOOOOONK!

That's not right. We should be hearing heavenly trumpets, not the blare of a car horn...

A car horn...

It was then that the details of the scene before me solidified. I could make out the shape of Jonathan's range rover, the bonnet all bent and mangled, in the middle of the room, with bits of brick and wood and building piled around it. Behind it, a huge, jagged hole opened the room to the world outside.

"I'll be damned," Heathcliff growled as he struggled to his knees, his chest heaving as he breathed in the fresh air pouring into the hole.

"Birdie..." Morrie gasped.

Quoth shoved his head out the window, waving at us from across the debris. "Jonathan was right about something – a diesel engine will save the day."

CHAPTER THIRTY-THREE

*Q*uoth ran to me, tucked me under his arms, and dragged me out the hole he'd created, onto the sodden lawn. I gasped at the fresh air. Shards of ice stabbed at my lungs, but I was so grateful for the pain. I could feel because I was *alive*.

Thanks to Quoth.

"You…" I rasped, struggling to speak. "You saved me…again."

"Always." He kissed the top of my head. "I'll always find a way to you in the darkness."

I clung to him as I breathed and sobbed, so grateful for his warmth and his love and his ingenuity. Bitter cold rain pelted our bodies, sluicing away my tears before they even left my eyes.

Quoth stroked my hair. "Are you okay if I leave you? I don't want to, but I need to get Morrie and Heathcliff and Donna. They're still too weak to move."

"Yes. Go…"

Quoth lowered me against the earth, placing my body in the recovery position, probably in case I passed out. I lay shivering in the muddy grass, sucking in life-giving air, hacking and coughing as my body discharged the poison, when lightning lit up the sky and I noticed a dark shape moving across the edge of the fields.

"It's Jonathan!" I yelled, although I think all that came out was a croak. "He's getting away."

"No, he won't," Heathcliff cried. His white robe flapped as he ran past me, taking off after Jonathan with a heavy object in his hand – Morrie's ceremonial sword. Heathcliff grasped Quoth's arm as he passed, and Quoth leaped after him, transforming into his bird midair and soaring ahead of Heathcliff.

But I couldn't see any way they would catch him. Jonathan was far away from the house, and not even Heathcliff would be able to close the distance between them. And Jonathan knew the estate better than anyone. Once he and Fergus entered the trees, they'd be able to escape.

But Heathcliff didn't chase after Jonathan. He veered off the path, and he and Quoth barreled toward a dark structure.

The aviary.

Quoth's voice rang clear in the night, his croaking cries heard above the wailing wind. I couldn't understand what he was telling the other ravens, but they clamored in reply. Heathcliff cried out as he fell upon the doors, hammering the pommel of the sword into the lock. With the power cut off, all he had to do was break the unit. He flung the door open and several dark shapes swooped past his head and took to the skies.

Quoth joined the unkindness, swooping low, croaking instructions. They soared across the lawn, majestic and terrifying as they went after their captor. All I could make out were majestic black specks swooping and dancing as they battled the storm. They dived into the trees. A moment later, Jonathan's scream tore through the night.

Fergus came running out of the trees, straight into Heath-cliff's arms. "Don't worry, boy." Heathcliff hugged the dog. "You're safe now."

CHAPTER THIRTY-FOUR

$\mathcal{M}$orrie stayed with me, his arms around me in an attempt to ward off the chill, while Heathcliff and Quoth dragged Jonathan's prone body back to the house. Before our eyes, the lights in all the rooms flickered to life, and a purring sound rose from one of the outbuildings. Someone got the generator working.

"Is he alive?"

"For his sins," Heathcliff grunted as they lifted the heavy groundskeeper up the steps to the restaurant. "When he wakes up, he'll wish he wasn't."

"Let that be a lesson to never piss off a raven." Quoth dropped Jonathan's legs on the carpet. Heathcliff dragged Jonathan into the private dining room where he'd trapped us only an hour before. Quoth had grabbed his clothes from the library and put them back on so that no one would ask why he was wandering around naked.

Heathcliff tied Jonathan's hands with a curtain tie, removed all the swords, and locked the door behind him. We gathered in the restaurant, where several guests and the other writers were congregating after they heard the noise and felt the shudder of the car driving through the library.

"Well, I'll be damned," Charlie said as Heathcliff filled him in on what had happened. "It was the groundskeeper all along. That Jonathan sure had us all fooled."

"Not Mina," Heathcliff's voice dripped with pride as he hugged me into his fluffy robe. "She put it all together. Not so bad for an amateur, is it?"

Charlie seemed to melt under Heathcliff's glare. "That's v-v-very impressive, Mina," he murmured as he backed away. "I take back everything I said earlier about amateur sleuths. If you'll excuse me, I have to go over there now for...for the safety of my testicles."

"Damn right," Heathcliff growled as Charlie pushed his way through the crowd.

"I can't believe you got that tiny car through the wall!" Christina rubbed my freezing fingers between hers.

"When I was outside, I noticed that Jonathan left his keys in the range rover," Quoth said modestly. "Not even an ancient castle wall is any match for that beast of a vehicle."

"First thing when I get back to Argleton, I'm buying one," said Morrie. "No, make that three!"

"Over my dead body," Heathcliff muttered.

"It can be arranged," Morrie shot back.

"That was so brave," Christina gushed, turning to Quoth with a note of desire in her voice. "It's so rare to meet a man who is both brave *and* handsome. Killian is neither, which is why I'm dumping him as soon as we get out of here. So I'll be single, just so you know."

I couldn't help but burst out laughing at Quoth's miserable face. I rolled my engagement ring around my finger.

"But how did you know that Mina, Heathcliff, and Morrie were trapped inside the library?" Vivianne interrupted. "None of us could hear a thing through those thick walls."

"Oh, well, I—"

"And your shirt is on inside out." Christina reached for Quoth's buttons. "Let me fix that for you."

"That's okay, please—"

"Make room," Morrie yelled as he staggered into the restaurant, carrying Donna. Heathcliff swept the china off one of the tables and Morrie laid her down, cradling her head and whispering something in her ear that made her bolt upright.

"I'm okay." She looked all around. "What happened? All I remember was walking toward the bathroom, and something hit me on the back of the head..."

"Jonathan tried to kill you," I said. "He murdered Hugh, too, because you stole his manuscript and Hugh was going to publish it. He tried to kill me and my fiancés, but Allan managed to stop him by driving a car through the wall of the library."

"I hope you've got a good contractor," Heathcliff said. "Because there's a gaping hole in the side of the castle."

Donna looked utterly flummoxed. "But..."

"And you should probably forget about publishing that manuscript," Morrie added. "Stealing the words of another writer is an unforgivable crime, unless they're in the public domain and you turn their villainous characters into dishy romance heroes, then it's totally fine."

"But...why are ravens sitting in the windows? And what's that?" Donna pointed a trembling finger at the stain on the carpet from where Heathcliff and Quoth dragged Jonathan inside. "Is that blood?"

"Yes."

When Heathcliff didn't elaborate, Donna clutched her hand to her forehead. She looked like she might faint again. But then, Vivianne stepped forward.

"This has been an appalling weekend. You'll be hearing from my lawyer," Vivianne grumbled.

"And mine," Charlie piped up from the back of the room.

"And I'm only giving this hotel three stars on Tripadvisor," Killian added.

"Three stars? For a murder?" Vivianne sounded appalled.

Killian shrugged. "The mud wrap was *excellent*."

"I thought it was all kind of fun," Christina said brightly, throwing her arms around me. "I mean, not the murder part, but the rest of it. I'm so pleased you're okay, Mina. Just think, we were part of a real-life murder mystery!"

"Trust me, the novelty wears off," I grumbled.

"Admit it, you love this," Quoth said as he helped me into a seat at a nearby table.

"Okay, fine. I admit that I did really enjoy being right about who the murderer is." I shuddered. "But I never, ever want to be poisoned by natural gas ever again."

"I am also not a fan," Morrie added. "If anyone's air is cut off, it should only be for a kinky sex game—"

"I smell bacon." My stomach grumbled as I sniffed the air. I could hear sounds from the kitchen of an early breakfast being rustled up. My mouth watered. It had to be like 3AM in the morning, but I was suddenly so starving.

"And black pudding." Heathcliff's voice rumbled with happiness.

"And those tiny sausages!" Morrie cried gleefully.

Quoth stroked my hand. "Can someone get our fiancée something to eat?"

Fiancée.

I held up my hand to the light, admiring the glittering stones and the twisted metal vine that held them together. In all the chaos, I'd almost forgotten that the guys proposed to me in the library.

And I accepted.

I, Mina Wilde, amateur sleuth, vampire slayer, bookshop co-owner, and blind girl about town, was officially engaged to the three most wonderful men in the world. Men who shouldn't even exist outside of storybooks, but who found me when I needed them most and have proven time and time again that they will always, always have my back and bring me bacon.

I nuzzled my head into Quoth's shoulder. "I'm so sorry."

"What for?"

"For doubting you." I peered up at Morrie before settling my gaze on Heathcliff's stormy features. "For suspecting you all of being murderers when really you were creating this romantic proposal for me."

"It doesn't matter." Heathcliff bent down and kissed me with surprising tenderness. "Morrie was right to laugh. When I think of the way we were acting, of course you would suspect us. From the night we found Ashley's body in the shop, you've been learning to believe in the impossible and to question everything."

"I feel awful. I should never have doubted you."

"Gorgeous, let's get this straight right now." Morrie plonked down in the seat opposite me. He reached across the table and held my hands in his. "You had one thing right – I *will* knock the head off anyone who wrongs you."

"Not if I get there first," Heathcliff growled.

"We will do *anything* to protect you, Mina. Anything. And so it doesn't bother us that you thought we'd bumped Briston off. Honestly, we might've done it if you hadn't asked us not to. He was an awful man and the publishing world is better off without him."

"Hear, hear!" Vivianne cried as she set down a plate of food in front of me. "Hugh is gone forever and I've still got my publishing deal, so everything has worked out perfectly in the end. Eat up, my dear. There's plenty more where that came from."

*W*e were halfway through our second heaping of bacon, hash browns, black pudding, eggs, tomatoes, and sausages when Donna staggered into the restaurant and announced that the mobile network was working again.

"Repair crews are up on the road. They must have fixed the issue with the tower," she said. "I've just got off the phone with the police. They're sending a car up here immediately to arrest Jonathan and remove Hugh's body, as well as a rescue crew to clear the road."

Everyone broke into loud applause.

"It's been a crazy night, and I thank you all for your patience and understanding, and I hope that you won't hold the events against Meddleworth or my staff. My team will be coming around with free spa vouchers for everyone. And Mina, thank you." Donna reached down and clasped my hand. "You and your boyfriends saved my life. And without you, we would still be trapped in that dining room, blaming each other for the murder, when it was that wretch Jonathan all along."

I tried to smile, but I was sure it came out as more than a grimace.

"I have to get back to work. There's lots to do. Enjoy your breakfast." Donna broke away from the group and I heard her on her mobile phone, giving an interview with the press while she used a second phone to snap pictures of the ravens and the hole in the wall for the 'gram. She got a second call, and when she heard it was the BBC, she actually *squealed* with delight.

The woman was almost murdered because she stole Jonathan's manuscript so she could make money off Meddleworth, and now here she was, trying to spin the story to raise the profile of the estate and spa.

Somehow, I doubted that Donna Bollstead had learned anything from the weekend's events.

"Mina, I came by to wish you well. I'm off now. I'm going to help the rescue crew manage traffic on the road." Charlie Doyle nodded to us as he passed our table. Beside me, Heathcliff stiffened, but I placed my hand over his.

"Thank you," I said. "I wish you well, too. What are you going to do now?"

"I'm going to pull out of the Red Herring contract and take my book elsewhere. I didn't work on that manuscript for ten years to have someone rewrite it for me. I want to see my own words between the pages. Otherwise, it's a hollow achievement. Good luck with everything, Mina. I might not have liked your book, but even I can concede you're one hell of a detective."

I beamed. *Oh, Charlie, you have* no *idea.*

CHAPTER THIRTY-FIVE

"*I*'m sad to see her go." Morrie's voice was heaped with sorrow as we watched (well, they watched, I listened) a tow truck crunch down the driveway, carting away the mangled wreckage of Jonathan's range rover and Morrie's little Leaf to their final resting place.

"I hope you've learned your lesson," Heathcliff. "Electric cars and criminal masterminds from the 1800s don't mix."

"That's a matter of opinion. James Moriarty has had his first taste of the freedom of being behind the wheel, and he's never giving it up." He grinned. "When we get back to Argleton, I'm going for my pilot's license."

"You will *not*. You'll die, and then who will buy the expensive French wine?"

"Don't be such a sourpuss worrypants. I'll be *fine*." Morrie waved a hand dismissively at the sky. "Look at that huge expanse of blue. There's way less to crash into up there. Come then, we'd better not be late for the bus."

"Yes." I hoisted my bag a little higher on my shoulder. "Let's get back to Nevermore. I want to see if Grimalkin's okay."

~

*CW*e arrived back in Argleton four hours later, tired and grumpy and smelling of the salted peanuts Morrie brought along for a snack and accidentally spilled in my Vivienne Westwood purse. (Not that I'm bitter or anything. Not at all.)

"It's got smaller," Quoth said as we stared up at the shop.

"Agreed. It's positively cramped." Morrie turned to Heathcliff. "Why don't we live in a castle with a moat and a spa again?"

Heathcliff made a face. "At least it's still in one piece. That Bree is not so terrible. As long as her oaf of a centurion didn't put any sword holes in the walls."

"You're one to talk," I smiled, thinking of Heathcliff's sword quivering in the library wall.

The door flung open. "Mina, you're back!" Bree ran down the steps and threw her arms around me, then picked up my suitcase and started dragging it inside. "I have a surprise for you."

"I spoke too soon," Heathcliff muttered as he followed us into the shop.

"Is Grimalkin okay?" I asked. "I've been worried about her. I'm sorry I didn't reply to your texts. Things at Meddleworth got a little murder-y."

"That's cool, and yeah, she's fine. But...come on!"

Intrigued, I directed Oscar to follow Bree through the shop to our apartment on the second floor. Bree had tidied up a little and stoked the fire, filling the room with warmth.

"That cat better not be sitting on my chair," Heathcliff grumbled as he staggered toward his favorite seat.

Bree blocked him with her body. "Just have a look before you sit down."

I ducked around Heathcliff and leaned over the arm of the chair. There, wrapped in a cozy blanket and smirking like the Queen of Sheba herself, was Grimalkin.

But she wasn't alone.

Six tiny, furry kittens wriggled beside her, fighting for milk.

"Omigooooooods..." I cooed as I reached out to stroke one on the cheek. "When did this happen?"

"Late last night," Bree said, kneeling beside me and patting Grimalkin's head. "When I took her to the vet, she said that Grimalkin wasn't sick. Or obese. She was pregnant. So I made her a nice warm bed and she did a splendid job. A real trooper."

I laughed. "I can't believe we didn't notice she was pregnant."

"I guess it never occurred to us," Quoth said, sitting on the rug. One of the kittens rolled off the edge of the chair and Quoth caught it in his hands, bringing the tiny, black ball of fluff to his cheek and nuzzling it.

"To be fair, we didn't know that shapeshifting cats who are really ancient nymphs could get pregnant," I said as I cradled a tiny black-and-white kitten in my hands. It made little 'meep' sounds as its tiny claws kneaded my thumb.

"Aren't these kittens quite advanced?" Heathcliff asked. "Newborn kittens shouldn't be able to see, hear, or walk."

I regarded him with interest.

"Not that I know anything about kittens," he added quickly. "Bloody annoying little things."

I glance at my grandmother, who had rolled on her back, luxuriating in our attention. "Could it be her magic? The babies must've inherited some of hers? It would be just like Grimalkin to make her babies age faster so she didn't have to mother them so much.

"Mew." Grimalkin shoots me a look that clearly says, *I resent that. I'm an excellent mother.*

"I didn't take the kittens back to the vet for that reason," Bree said. "I figured it was just another strange occurance at Nevermore Bookshop."

A bright-eyed girl with tabby stripes broke away from her brothers and sisters and struck out boldly toward a stack of books on the side table. She prodded gingerly at a copy of *A Room of One's Own* before giving it a delighted nudge with he paws and sending it sliding across the floor. She tumbled after it and started chewing on the corner.

"You're a little adventuress." I moved the book away and she leaped after it on tiny, shaking legs. "I'm going to name you Woolf. After Virginia Woolf."

"Great, now she's naming them." Heathcliff huffed. "If you name them, then we can't give them away—"

"Reeeeeeeooooowww…" Grimalkin hissed what she thought of that idea.

"Arf," Oscar added. He sniffed the kittens, excited to have new friends.

"Of course we're giving them away. How could you do this to us?" Heathcliff glowered at Grimalkin.

"Meow!"

"As if this shop isn't already a menagerie of chaos, what with the dogs and cats and birds and customers, and now we're going to have six balls of fluff underfoot, tearing up the furniture, knocking over whisky bottles, and—"

Quoth dropped the black kitten into Heathcliff's hands.

Heathcliff's words died on his lips. He held his hands up to his face, his eyes widening and his frown softening as he watched the pitch-black kitten wriggle around in his arms.

"Squeak?" The kitten got right up close, leaned in, and bopped Heathcliff on the nose.

"Did you see that?" Heathcliff breathed.

"What's his name?" I asked.

"Maximillian," Heathcliff said immediately.

"If you name him, you're going to want to keep him," Morrie said with a smirk in his voice.

"Obviously, we're going to keep him. Who ever heard of such a barbarous thing as giving away Mina's grandmother's kittens? These are her aunts and uncles," Heathcliff said with complete sincerity. Maximilian clambered onto Heathcliff's shoulder and burrowed into his hair.

"Can I name this one Al Catone?" Morrie said, waving his finger for a little black-and-white boy. "He's wearing a tuxedo, so we're both impeccably dressed for villainy."

"And this one is Breeches," Heathcliff winced, turning around so we could all see the tiny calico bundle with its claws digging into his arse. Morrie burst out laughing.

"I think this guy is Phineas," Quoth said, as he pulled his hair aside to find a little ginger boy curled up asleep in there.

"You name this one," I told Bree, pointing to a little snowy-white madam who hadn't strayed far from her mother, and was glaring at all her brothers and sisters with disdain. "After all, if it wasn't for you helping her, Grimalkin might have had a difficult time. And Heathcliff's right, these kittens are family, and so are you."

"Meow." Grimalkin nodded her assent.

"Oh," Bree held the tiny girl in her hands. "Wow. Um, sure. What about Ghost? Edward says that when she was born, she kind of looked like a peanut. What do you think?"

"Peanut is perfect."

Woolf jumped on my shoelaces, and I hugged Bree and Quoth tight as I burst out laughing. Morrie ran to the kitchen and returned with a saucer of kitten milk and some treats for Grimalkin, and Heathcliff watched in wide-eyed awe as Maximillian wobbled his way down his arm like a tightrope walker.

Nevermore Bookshop was changing in more ways than one. And I couldn't be happier.

CHAPTER THIRTY-SIX

The next morning, I checked on Grimalkin and the kittens, helped Heathcliff to open up the shop, then went across the road to Nevermore Gallery. Quoth was hanging a series of paintings of landmarks around the village by a local watercolor artist. There were already a few tourists inside, browsing the bright artwork Quoth had hung on every surface. In the communal art space, two potters were bent over freshly fired bowls, painting designs with multi-colored glaze.

"To what do I owe the pleasure of seeing my fiancée before her second cup of coffee?" he teased as he folded me into his arms.

"I was going to go upstairs and get some writing done."

"Of course. I've left your studio all ready for you." Quoth tucked a strand of his obsidian hair behind his ear. "I'm happy to hear you're going to keep writing. After the nightmare of Meddleworth and Hugh Briston's retreat, I didn't think you'd want to pick up the pen again."

"Actually, the opposite is true. Ever since we got back, I've been itching to sit down and work on my book. Hugh may have been awful, but I did learn a few things from him. Plus, I've been texting Christina. She lives in London, and we think we might meet up some weekends to work on our drafts together."

"She's still talking to you, despite the whole suspecting her of being a murderer thing?"

"Women in literature should stick together," I said. "She said she was actually flattered that we considered her a suspect, and she thinks she might write a version of the whole ordeal in one of her future books."

"What about you?" Quoth leaned in close. "Will the Meddleworth locked-room mystery be part of a Mina Wilde story any time soon?"

"I don't know. Right now I'm just grateful to be far, far away from that castle." I brightened. "Oh, and Christina has decided to self-publish her latest book. She thinks I should do it, too."

"Doesn't that mean selling your books through The-Store-That-Shall-Not-be-Named?" Heathcliff growled as he and Morrie poked their heads through the door. "To people who read ebooks?"

"Hey, ebooks are great," I said. I'd been reading on a Kindle ever since my eyesight started to get worse. Now I read mainly audiobooks, which Heathcliff also had many rants about. "And Christina told me that I'd be able to print paperback copies that we could sell in the store. She made it sound pretty cool, actually."

"Mina Wilde, published author." Quoth wrapped his arms around me. "It has a nice ring to it."

"It does. But I actually think I'm going to use a pseudonym. The story is too close to our real life – I don't want people to get the wrong idea about us, or to suspect any of it is real and take you away for testing." I shuddered at the thought of anyone hurting Quoth. "And I really, *really* don't want my mother reading all those intimate sex scenes."

"Oooh, a faux identity under which you can get up to all kinds of shenanigans." Morrie rubbed his hands together with glee. "Can we make suggestions?"

"No suggestions." I folded my arms and glared in his direction. "Shouldn't you all be back at the shop? I saw tons of people coming in."

"We're surplus to requirements," Morrie said. "Everyone's come to see the kittens."

"They're not for sale," Heathcliff growled.

Grumpy, surly Heathcliff has really warmed to our chaotic, animal-filled life.

"No one's buying anything, and Grimalkin's holding court in her human form, annoying the bejeezus out of Heathcliff, so we're going to Oliver's for pastries."

"And kitten milk," Heathcliff added.

"Oooh, pastries!" I perked up. "Bring us back some. But don't think you can slack off today. You have work to do."

"What work?"

"I've got a book deadline and we're getting married in three months." I handed Heathcliff a thick, bright pink planning folder. "You'd better get cracking. You have a wedding to plan."

TO BE CONTINUED

Wedding bells are ringing in Nevermore Bookshop, but Mina's got more than seating charts and cake mishaps to worry about when the priest turns up dead. Will our foursome be able to tie the knot amongst the chaos and carnage? Find out in the final book in the Nevermore Bookshop Mysteries – *Plot and Bothered.*

READ NOW

http://books2read.com/plotandbothered

〜

What do you do when 3 hot, possessive ghosts want to jump your bones? Find out in Bree's series, the Grimdale Graveyard Mysteries, and enjoy cameos from your favourite characters from Nevermore Bookshop.

START NOW:
http://books2read.com/grimdale1

(Turn the page for a sizzling excerpt)

Can't get enough of Mina and her boys? Read a free alternative scene from Quoth's point-of-view along with other bonus scenes and extra stories when you sign up for the Steffanie Holmes newsletter.

http://www.steffanieholmes.com/newsletter

FROM THE AUTHOR

Welcome back to Nevermore Bookshop. I know it's been a while since we stepped through the front door to meet a grumpy, love-able giant, a suave and cheeky criminal genius, and a beautiful and kind raven – and let us not forget the stuffed armadillo.

I wrote this book while my country, New Zealand, was battered by Cyclone Gabrielle. One of our solar panels caught fire, the roof of my greenhouse tore off (we still don't know where it went), and my parents – who live in the most harshly impacted area – went AWOL for three days. It was A TIME.

But having Mina, Heathcliff, Morrie, and Quoth for company kept me sane. From the very beginning I knew I wanted to tackle a locked-room mystery, but the cyclone gave me the inspiration for the storm that trapped Mina and her fellow writers inside Meddleworth. I definitely wish my house had a spa, though.

So often I hear from readers about how much they love this series, and it gives them a safe, warm, cozy feeling. I love that! I get the same feeling when I write the books. I hope you enjoy *Crime & Publishing* as much as I adored writing it. And I hope you're ready for the series finale with *Plot and Bothered*.

And if you need something to help you deal with your Nevermore book hangover, I've got you covered. Check out the Grimdale Graveyard Mysteries series, where our heroine Bree is up to her ears in ghostly shenanigans with her harem of three possessive spirits. Book 1 is *You're So Dead to Me* and it's set in the same world as Nevermore, so you'll meet a few of your favourite characters: http://books2read.com/grimdale1

If you want to hang out and talk about all things Nevermore, get updates and a free book of cut scenes and bonus stories, you can join my newsletter – http://steffanieholmes.com/newsletter.

A portion of the proceeds from every Nevermore book sold go toward supporting Blind Low Vision NZ Guide Dogs, and I'm always sharing cute guide dog pictures and vids in my Facebook group.

I'm so happy you enjoyed this story! I'd love it if you wanted to leave a review on Amazon or Goodreads. It will help other readers to find their next read.

Thank you, thank you! I love you heaps! Until next time.
Steffanie

YOU'RE SO DEAD TO ME IS OUT NOW!

READ A BRAND NEW KOOKY, SPOOKY PARANORMAL SERIES SET IN THE WORLD OF NEVERMORE

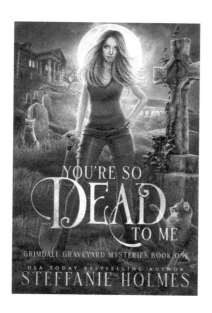

What do you do when three hot, possessive ghosts want to jump your bones?

I'm Bree, and I see dead people.

Not all dead people. Only those with unfinished business. They're everywhere – I'll be eating my breakfast and a poisoned heiress glares over my Cheerios, and I can't even enjoy the wilderness without being accosted by chattering ex-hikers who don't understand which mushrooms are edible.

I've returned to my hometown of Grimdale to cat-sit for my parents while I plan my next move. I'm looking forward to raiding their fridge, hanging out with their two mischievous kittens, and staying far, far away from anything supernatural.

But I forgot that I'm never alone in Grimdale.

The three ghosts I used to play with as a kid are back in my life again. Only now I'm their age and they're *infuriatingly* attractive.

There's the *slightly* psychotic Roman soldier who loves the Great British Bake Off, the bossy, aristocratic royal prince who demands the finer things in life (er, death), and the blind Victorian gentleman adventurer who doesn't have a mean bone in his body (or any bones, for that matter).

But my three ghoulish houseguests are the least of my problems. I've landed a job giving tours of the historic Grimdale Cemetery, and on my very first day, I stumble into a fresh corpse.

The dead guy's ghost needs me to solve his murder so he can cross over, but sticking my nose into spirit business might see me to an early grave.

As for my three hauntingly hot friends? It turns out their unfinished business…is me.

You're So Dead to Me is the first in a darkly humorous paranormal romance series by bestselling author Steffanie Holmes. If you love a sarcastic heroine, hot, possessive and slightly unhinged ghostly men, a mystery to solve, and a little kooky, spooky lovin' to set your coffin a rockin', then quit ghouling around and start reading!

READ NOW:

http://books2read.com/grimdale1

Turn the page for a spooky excerpt:

EXCERPT

A DEAD AND STORMY NIGHT

Start the Grimdale Graveyard Mysteries series and dive into a new adventure in the same world as Nevermore Bookshop: http://books2read.com/grimdale1

"Go on, dearie. Let me have a little sniff of that salty goodness."

"No," I snap under my breath as I snatch the pretzels from the tray table and stuff them in my pocket.

For your information, I'm not hanging out in the world's grossest sex club. (That was two years ago in Amsterdam. My shoes stuck to the floor.) I'm sitting in my seat on a flight somewhere over the United Arab Emirates, minding my own business and trying to ignore the ghost of a blue-haired old biddy who is annoyingly fascinated by my airline snacks.

"Pleeeeease? Just hold the bag out so I can have a whiff."

I glare at her before turning my body toward the window. Outside, the world is dark – the kind of deep, unsettling darkness that makes you remember you're hurtling through space at a gazillion miles an hour with only a computer, a hopefully not-drunk pilot, and the laws of physics standing between you and a fiery, dramatic death. We're somewhere over the Middle East, but the cloud cover is so thick that it looks like we're flying into a black hole.

Most people in the cabin are settling down to sleep, but I won't get any peace as long as Chatty Cathy insists on a running commentary of my snacks.

"I know you can see me, dearie," she sighs. I watch out of the corner of my eye as she hovers over the empty seat beside me. "My good friend the headless pilot told me all about you. Well, he didn't tell me so much as gesticulated. He said your thighs were much bigger. You should eat more, put some meat on those bones – starting with those pretzels in your pocket."

I groan. Stupid ghosts. They have no right to be gesticulating about the size of my thighs, which are perfectly fine as they are, thank you very much.

It figures that airplane ghosts talk to each other. There aren't that many of them compared to, say, hospitals, old asylums, and Starbucks stores. They generally stick to the plane where they died but they can hop off at airports and float around in the terminals like some kind of spectral hen party, swapping gossip about their flights. The Headless Pilot and I had a run-in on my flight from Bali last year, and it was not a pleasant experience. I was on the loo, reading a smutty romance novel on my phone and enjoying hour three of *absolutely no dead people* when he stuck his torso through the bathroom door and shook his neck stub at me. I screamed bloody murder because that's what you do when you have a see-through neck stub in your face, and the stewardess had to break down the door because she thought I was having some kind of fit. They didn't believe my story about seeing a spider, and I've been banned from that airline for life.

Ghosts are nothing but trouble.

Usually, airplanes are one of the few places in the world where I'm blissfully free of ghosts for a while. Statistically, not that many people die on planes. It's one of the reasons I decided to leave my small British village of Grimdale the moment I got my GCSE and embark on a backpacking trip around the world. It wasn't the most pressing motivation, but it definitely factored high on my 'reasons to get as far from Grimdale as possible' list.

And now, after all this time, I'm heading *back* to Grimdale, a place I very much do not want to be, because of the terrible thing...

No. I squeeze my eyes shut. *I don't want to think about that. If I burst into tears on this plane, Chatty Cathy will never let me hear the end of it.*

"Excuse me, ma'am?"

I open my eyes and see the reflection of a man in a business suit in the window. Ghosts don't have reflections, so it's a real live person talking to me. That doesn't happen often – my resting bitchface is so legendary that sonnets have been composed in its honor.

I spin around. Businessman McArmaniPants flashes me an apologetic smile. He leans forward and puts his arm on the back of the seat, right through the old lady's spectral head.

"Argh, watch where you're putting those skinbags, you rotten oaf!" She jerks away, holding her head as she hops angrily down the aisle. She looks like a chicken with her bony elbows jerking wildly. I cough into my hand to cover my smirk.

Businessman McArmaniPants flashes me a megawatt smile. "I didn't mean to startle you. I noticed that this seat is empty. I wondered if I could sit next to you – I'm near the back and a kid spilled his orange juice and now everything is sticky—"

"Sure." I pat the seat, grateful for his presence. He'll act as a buffer between me and the old lady ghost. "Please, make yourself at home. Stay as long as you like."

"Do not make yourself at home!" Chatty Cathy huffs, glaring at the man as he lowers himself into her seat. "This is my chair. I claimed it first. Get your own snacks to sniff."

"Do you want some pretzels?" I crack open the bag and offer

it to my new seatmate, knowing that the ghost won't want to risk getting close enough to sniff them now.

"Sure." He takes a handful. "Hey, why are you poking out your tongue?"

"Oh." A blush creeps across my cheeks as the old biddy huffs away. "No reason."

Are you ready for a little ghost lore? I'm on the second leg of my thirty-two hours of flying from New Zealand to London, so I have time to kill.

Time to kill. Ha ha. I'm a comedian.

Here's the skinny on the spirits of the dead, aka, Bree's Ghost Rules:

1. Not everyone who dies becomes a ghost. You have to have unfinished business. Often, you don't remember what that business is, which I'm sure must be annoying.
2. Ghosts hang around the location where they died. There's an invisible force I call ghost mojo (it's a highly technical term I came up with when I was eight, shut up) that acts like a rubber band that pulls them back to the location of their death. They can wander away from their death location, but the ghost mojo gets worse the further they go until it becomes painful for them to remain away and they get sucked back to their death place again.
3. Some ghosts, like my childhood friend Ambrose, aren't tied to a death location but instead, a place that's important to them. I don't know how it works, so I blame it on ghost mojo.

4. Ghost mojo is also why ghosts can fly through airplane bathroom doors but don't fall through the floor and out into space. Ghost mojo keeps spirits standing on the ground the way they did when they were alive.

5. Only very powerful or very angry ghosts can interact with the human world by moving things or flickering lights or writing on mirrors. Mostly they just waft around being annoying.

6. Despite not having noses, they can still sense strong smells, so they're forever lingering around when people are eating and begging to sniff my salty nuts.

7. Ghosts hate it when humans walk through them. *Hate. It.* Sometimes I do it just because I know it pisses them off so much.

How do I know so much about ghosts?

Because I'm the only person who can see them.

I had an accident when I was five years old – I fell off my bike and cracked my head on a rock – and ever since I've been able to see the dead. See them and talk to them and be infinitely harassed by them—

"Go on, dearie," the old lady pokes her head out of the luggage rack. "Just a little sniff."

I'm Bree Mortimer. And it's going to be a long flight.

TO BE CONTINUED

Start reading the Grimdale Graveyard Mysteries series now:
http://books2read.com/grimdale1

OTHER BOOKS BY STEFFANIE HOLMES

Nevermore Bookshop Mysteries

A Dead and Stormy Night

Of Mice and Murder

Pride and Premeditation

How Heathcliff Stole Christmas

Memoirs of a Garroter

Prose and Cons

A Novel Way to Die

Much Ado About Murder

Crime and Publishing

Plot and Bothered

Grimdale Graveyard Mysteries

What do you do when three hot AF, possessive ghosts want to jump your bones? Find out in this spooky, kooky paranormal romance series set in the same world as Nevermore Bookshop.

You're So Dead To Me

If You've Got It, Haunt It

Ghoul as a Cucumber

Not a Mourning Person

Kings of Miskatonic Prep

Shunned

Initiated

Possessed

Ignited

Stonehurst Prep

My Stolen Life

My Secret Heart

My Broken Crown

My Savage Kingdom

Stonehurst Prep Elite

Poison Ivy

Poison Flower

Poison Kiss

DARK ACADEMIA

Pretty Girls Make Graves

Brutal Boys Cry Blood

Manderley Academy

Ghosted

Haunted

Spirited

Briarwood Witches

Earth and Embers

Fire and Fable

Water and Woe

Wind and Whispers

Spirit and Sorrow

Crookshollow Gothic Romance

Art of Cunning (Alex & Ryan)

Art of the Hunt (Alex & Ryan)

Art of Temptation (Alex & Ryan)

The Man in Black (Elinor & Eric)

Watcher (Belinda & Cole)

Reaper (Belinda & Cole)

Wolves of Crookshollow

Digging the Wolf (Anna & Luke)

Writing the Wolf (Rosa & Caleb)

Inking the Wolf (Bianca & Robbie)

Wedding the Wolf (Willow & Irvine)

Want to be informed when the next Steffanie Holmes paranormal romance story goes live? Sign up for the newsletter at www.steffanieholmes.com/newsletter to get the scoop, and score a free collection of bonus scenes and stories to enjoy!

ABOUT THE AUTHOR

Steffanie Holmes is the *USA Today* bestselling author of the paranormal, gothic, dark, and fantastical. Her books feature clever, witty heroines, secret societies, creepy old mansions and alpha males who *always* get what they want.

Legally-blind since birth, Steffanie received the 2017 Attitude Award for Artistic Achievement. She was also a finalist for a 2018 Women of Influence award.

Steff is the creator of *Rage Against the Manuscript* – a resource of free content, books, and courses to help writers tell their story, find their readers, and build a badass writing career.

Steffanie lives in New Zealand with her husband, a horde of cantankerous cats, and their medieval sword collection.

STEFFANIE HOLMES NEWSLETTER

Grab a free copy of *Cabinet of Curiosities* – a Steffanie Holmes compendium of short stories and bonus scenes – when you sign up for updates with the Steffanie Holmes newsletter.

http://www.steffanieholmes.com/newsletter

Come hang with Steffanie
www.steffanieholmes.com
hello@steffanieholmes.com

Milton Keynes UK
Ingram Content Group UK Ltd.
UKHW041303111123
432394UK00001B/33